Y0-DAD-794

"This is my place and you live by *my* rules..."

"...It's either that." He seethed while taking the gun from its holster. "Or you can die by them."

As soon as Barstow went for his gun, the entire saloon erupted in chaos. Clint could hear the footsteps closing in behind him as though they were the only noise in the room. ... With his left hand, Clint reached out to snatch the gun away from Barstow just as the rich man pulled the trigger. Clint tightened his grip around the weapon, putting the base of his thumb beneath the hammer so that the firing pin lodged into his flesh rather than set off a round into the deputy's face.

By the time the blood started trickling down Clint's hand, he pushed the chair back and was on his feet. ... Clint pointed each of the guns he'd taken back at their owners and stood so that he was positioned directly between the men.

"All right now," Clint said calmly. "Let's just stop and think about this before things get too out of hand."

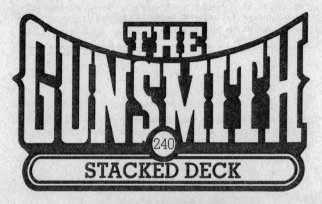

THE GUNSMITH

240

STACKED DECK

J. R. ROBERTS

JOVE BOOKS, NEW YORK

STACKED DECK

A Jove Book / published by arrangement with
the author

PRINTING HISTORY
Jove edition / December 2001

All rights reserved.
Copyright © 2001 by Robert J. Randisi.
This book, or parts thereof, may not be reproduced in any form
without permission.
For information address: The Berkley Publishing Group,
a division of Penguin Putnam Inc.,
375 Hudson Street, New York, New York 10014.

Visit our website at
www.penguinputnam.com

ISBN: 0-515-13207-1

A JOVE BOOK®
Jove Books are published by The Berkley Publishing Group,
a division of Penguin Putnam Inc.,
375 Hudson Street, New York, New York 10014.
JOVE and the "J" design
are trademarks belonging to Penguin Putnam Inc.

PRINTED IN THE UNITED STATES OF AMERICA

10 9 8 7 6 5 4 3 2 1

ONE

Clint Adams had been in the cold weather for so long that he swore he had ice running through his veins. The last several months had been filled with nothing but frozen winds, iced landscapes and mountains of snow. As much as he'd tried to get out of the cold and head for warmer climates, he'd been dragged back into it by some turn of events or another kind of crisis.

And all the while, the gambling part of Clint's mind kept telling him to be patient and sit tight until his luck changed. He'd been in more than enough poker games to know that even the worst stretches of bad luck came to an end, eventually. All that mattered was that a man had enough of a stake to make it to the winning hands.

Finally, after what had seemed like an eternity of numb fingers and frozen toes, Clint made it across the Colorado border into New Mexico. The farther south he went, the better it felt. It wasn't anything that struck him immediately, but after a while he'd started shrugging off his jacket and shedding the layers of wool that had been his second skin for so very long.

The gloves came off his hands, and when the snow finally gave way to soil and sand, he could fully appreciate the feel of the sun on his back. Its rays washed over him like a warm, soothing massage to loosen his muscles and add some color to his skin. Even Eclipse seemed to be walking quicker. The

Darley Arabian stallion had pulled through just fine during the trek through the snow, almost as though it had forgotten what warmer weather felt like. Now that his hide wasn't half frozen, Eclipse was more partial to trotting rather than a slow walk.

Rather than try to rein in the stallion, Clint let Eclipse go until he ran himself down. The horse's energy must have been infectious because Clint felt like climbing down from the saddle so he could stretch his own legs.

His boots sunk into the sand just enough to warm the soles of his feet, a feeling that seemed strange after fighting back frostbite for the last few months. The part of New Mexico he was in wasn't quite desert, but it was close enough to make any man cautious—even a man who welcomed the heat like a long-lost friend.

Retrieving the canteen from one of his saddlebags, Clint unscrewed the top and poured some of the water down his throat. It washed the trail dust away, but didn't do half as good a job as a cold beer. He cupped his hand and poured some water into it.

"Here you go, boy," Clint said as he put his hand to Eclipse's mouth.

The horse lapped up the moisture with a few flicks of its tongue and snorted approvingly.

"Thought we'd never make it out of the snow."

Looking ahead, Clint could see the trail winding down toward a small ravine lined with several scraggly trees. There were some mountains behind them and several bluffs in front of them. The sun was high in the sky, winking out occasionally as several thick banks of clouds rolled through on their way to dump rain on some of the towns farther south. Clint looked forward to seeing the rich colors of dusk later that night and even considered camping out under the stars even though he was fairly certain there was a town less than thirty miles or so down the trail.

He was headed toward a place called Modillo, which was a fairly large town a few miles east of Santa Fe. It was supposedly a great place to play cards and was usually hosting some kind of gambling tournament any time of the year.

All in all, it sounded like a good place to settle in and possibly win some of the money.

Clint was reminded about what had happened up in Colorado. Besides being the usual mess of people and their problems, the time had been particularly hard on the gun that had been with Clint long enough to be considered part of his family.

The modified Colt had taken a stray bullet, which put a nasty dent in its side; that was bad enough to keep it from firing properly. He'd managed to work around it at the time, but he certainly didn't like the prospect of riding much longer without fixing it. He'd spent plenty of time looking the pistol over and decided that although it wouldn't be hard to fix, it was something that would take some time. Clint had gotten started with some initial repairs over the last several nights and was anxious to sit down with the tools required to finish the job.

Modillo sounded like it was a big enough town that it would have someone there with the equipment he needed. It was either that or head all the way down to Labyrinth, Texas, where his old wagon was stored. He had plenty of tools there, but that would mean several more days of riding before the task was completed. Besides, the notion of taking his time and acquiring some newer tools appealed to Clint. It had been a while since he'd gotten a chance to practice his true craft.

Clint took another swig from the canteen and then placed it into his saddlebag before climbing onto Eclipse's back. With a flick of his wrists, he snapped the reins, which was all the stallion needed to be off and running once again. The hot wind was a smooth, tender caress across his cheeks, which even tasted good as it rolled into his nose and out his mouth.

He figured they should pull into Modillo by early evening. Already, Clint was thinking about how fine the beer would taste when accompanied by a thick, hearty steak. Even the prospect of playing cards made him want to get to town that much faster. It had been a while since he'd sat down to a good night of gambling and even longer since he'd had no one to worry about besides himself.

His experience told him that something would more than likely come up soon enough, but even that wasn't enough to dampen his spirits. At the very least, he could still feel the heat on his skin and couldn't see a single flake of snow. Everything else besides that was gravy.

Eclipse had been running full out for some time before the stallion finally started losing steam. Before the horse's breaths got too heavy, Clint reined him in and slowed down to a more leisurely pace. As fine a horse as the Darley was, he still didn't quite have the stamina of Clint's old black gelding, Duke. It was then that he heard something coming from a stretch of skeletal trees east of his position.

At first, it sounded as though a storm might have been brewing in the distance, but when he took another moment to listen harder, Clint could tell that what he'd heard was definitely not thunder. An uneasy feeling crept over him as he brought Eclipse to a stop and strained his ears for another hint.

It didn't take long before he picked up the sound again. It came from what looked like a smaller trail that hooked up with the one he was taking, about half a mile up. Pretty soon, he could see a cloud of dust forming that soon gave way to at least half a dozen riders charging toward the main trail.

The sounds Clint heard were unmistakable: the thundering of hooves on dry soil, raised voices and the crack of gunfire. More than that, he eventually saw something else at the front of the dust cloud: It was a single rider who was obviously doing his best to pull away from the ones doing the shooting.

Clint shook his head, not at all surprised that he'd come across a rampaging group of trigger-happy cowboys in the middle of a dry stretch of land. "Well," he said as he touched his heels to Eclipse's sides. "At least it's not snowing."

TWO

With the oncoming horses running as fast as their legs could carry them, Eclipse met up with them in less than a minute. As they got closer, Clint could hear the gunshots echoing through the air over the sound of beating hooves. He could also hear the hollering of men who pursued the single rider as though he was a prize quail.

Clint instinctively put his hand over his gun, but quickly remembered that it would be of no use to him if push came to shove. He was wearing his .32 Colt New Line hideaway tucked into his belt until he could get the gun fixed, but that wouldn't do any good over a distance of ground. Instead, he pulled the rifle from where it hung from his saddle and levered a round into the chamber. Rather than ride blindly into the fray, he stopped short and fired a round into the air.

With all the other guns going off, nobody seemed to notice Clint's rifle. Taking careful aim, he sighted down the barrel and squeezed the trigger again. This time, he sent a round just high enough over the lead cowboy's head to keep from drawing blood, but low enough to grab his attention.

In fact, that round seemed to grab all of their attention. Even the single rider trying to escape from the rest took a second to look around for the source of that last shot.

Once Clint saw the group of horses slow down and eventually stop, he brought Eclipse in a little closer with the rifle held across his lap. There were seven of them all together:

5

one who was running and six who were chasing. The runner wasted no time at all in making his way toward Clint with a grateful smile plastered across his face. An older man with a head full of long, scraggly gray hair, the runner had the look of a man who spent most of his life baking under the desert sun with the thick leathery hide to prove it. He stopped before getting too close, however, when he saw the deadly warning etched over Clint's features.

"What's going on here?" Clint asked.

The lead rider shifted in his saddle. A wiry man covered from head to toe in dust, the rider glared from atop his brown mare through a tight squint. Even from this distance, Clint could tell the other man's hand was itching to bring the pistol around in his direction. That impulse seemed to fade, however, as Clint adjusted the rifle so that it was pointing toward the entire group.

Without missing a beat, the rider who seemed to be in charge of the ones doing the chasing spoke up. "What we're doing ain't none of your business, mister."

"Are you men part of a posse?" Clint asked.

That question brought a wave of laughter through the small group. The leader's lips curled up in a leering smile to reveal a mouth half full of tobacco-stained teeth. "What kinda damn fool question is that?"

"It's the only sensible reason I could come up with for so many to be chasing down one man. Either that or you fellas don't believe in fair play."

"You're outgunned, mister. Just ride on and we'll forget we even crossed paths. Don't make me and my boys here teach you a hard lesson in the bad things that can happen when you don't tend to yer own affairs."

Clint moved his hand almost imperceptibly, shifting the rifle so that it was aimed directly at the man doing all the talking. When he had his sights set, he locked eyes with him and spoke loud enough for his voice to carry in every direction. "Let's just say that I get a bit nervous when I'm traveling. I see you chasing someone down like a dog with guns blazing and it gets me nervous. My mind starts to work and I think that after you catch what you're chasing that you might set your sights elsewhere. Maybe I'll be next.

"I've had a long ride. My horse is tired. I don't appreciate the thought of being chased any more than I like watching someone outnumbered by rowdy types like yourself. I prefer the quiet life. Then again, just in case I'm meddling where I'm not wanted, why don't I ask this man?" Turning toward the single rider, Clint asked, "How about it? Do you mind running from this group? Did I interrupt some strange way the locals here have of exercising their horses?"

Looking between Clint and the group of cowboys, the old man didn't quite seem to know which way to jump.

"Yeah," one of the other cowboys shouted. "What've you got to say, Ellis?"

Clint moved Eclipse closer to the old man. "Do you know these guys?"

When the old man nodded, it looked as though his neck had become unhinged from where it connected to his shoulders. "I know 'em, all right."

"Are they helping you exercise your horse?" Clint asked.

He took a moment, but eventually the old man shook his head. "No. They sure ain't."

Shifting his eyes back to glare fully into those of the cowboys' leader, Clint said, "Then why don't we all go our own ways before I get so nervous that my finger starts to twitch."

The man with the dirty smile kept still for a few seconds, eyeing Clint intently. Finally, he came to his decision. "Come on, boys," he said without looking away. "This old man ain't worth all this trouble. Besides," he added as he started turning his mare around, "we can catch up to him any time we feel like it."

Exploding into a noisy storm of pounding hooves and angry shouts, the cowboys rode south along the trail Clint had been taking. Even though there were plenty of curses thrown over their shoulders, not another shot was fired.

"Reckon I owe you some thanks, stranger," the old man said once the noise had died down a bit. Extending a hand between their two horses, he added, "The name's Ellis."

"I'm Clint." Once he was sure the others weren't going to double back just yet, Clint placed his rifle back into the leather strap on the side of his saddle. When he shook Ellis's hand, he was reminded of the smooth, tough hide of a lizard. "Lived around here long, Ellis?"

"Hell, I been a desert rat for m'whole life," the old man replied. Noticing that Clint had already started moving down the trail again, he brought his horse up alongside and kept pace. "Used to live in Arizona. Tombstone, in fact. But then there was some trouble in those parts that shook things up a little too much for my taste. You heard about all that mess?"

Clint's mind raced with memories of the time he'd spent in Tombstone. Ike Clanton and the McLowery's were feuding with the Earp brothers and Doc Holliday, which ended with a little ruckus at a place called the OK Corral. Clint had met up with Wyatt and Doc once or twice since then, but not for a while now.

"Yeah," Clint said. "I think I know what you're talking about."

"Well ever since I moved on into New Mexico, everything's been pretty quiet. I guess as quiet as a town as Modillo could ever be, anyway."

"What do you mean?"

"Modillo ain't exactly no sleepy little place, you know. What with the gambling houses and folks like Tannen living there, a man can see some excitement when he's spending time there."

Clint shook his head. "Is there as much excitement as you can see outside of town limits?"

At first, Ellis didn't seem to understand. Then his face reddened and he laughed nervously beneath his breath. "Oh . . . uh . . . I guess today would've been more well spent if I didn't go for my ride."

"So I take it that was Tannen who I met up with earlier?" Clint asked.

Ellis gave another loose nod. From this close, his skin looked dry enough to snap off when he moved that fast. Clint half expected the old man's bones to creak as he began gesturing wildly with his arms as he spoke.

"That was him all right," Ellis said. "Tannen's not the only one of his kind and he sure ain't the worst. He and them friends of his ride back and forth between here and Split Creek, robbin' some if they need the money and raisin' hell the whole way. I was just on my way there myself when I got stopped by that bunch. Thought I could outrun 'em with this here gelding. Might've done just that, too."

"I've never heard of Split Creek. Is it far from here?"

"It's a town about a day's ride east. Smaller than Modillo, but it's got just as much character."

"Character, huh?" Clint said as though the words tasted bad. "I guess that's one name for it."

THREE

The ride into Modillo was a short one. With Ellis talking in an endless stream of stories, jokes and tall tales, however, it seemed as though the trail would never come to an end. Finally, Clint caught sight of the town as they crested a ridge and he gave Eclipse a little extra nudge to get there that much faster.

Ellis seemed unaware of just how tired Clint had gotten and did his best to keep up with the Darley Arabian once it broke into a run. Surprisingly enough, Ellis's gelding held its own and soon they both rode into Modillo's limits.

Clint noticed immediately how busy the town seemed for its size. Although the place was no Dodge City or even a Tombstone, Modillo was larger than it had first appeared. It was arranged in the shape of a rectangle and seemed to get larger the deeper Clint rode within the streets. The sun was beginning to slip below the horizon, causing the town to light up like a glowing ember situated in the desert's grasp.

Ellis led Clint through the busy gambling district toward one of the town's two livery stables. Apparently, one was better than the other since it was built closer to a stream that created the town's southwestern border. Once there, Clint dismounted and led Eclipse into a large stable.

"This is as far as I can take you for now," Ellis said. "I live on the other end of town and if I stay around here too long the owner's son will tell my wife I'm still here instead

10

of in Split Creek. I'm hopin' to put in some time at the faro tables before that happens."

"Well, thanks for your help," Clint said while extending his hand.

Shaking hands, Ellis replied, "It's me that should thank you again. If you get the urge to whet your whistle later on, why don't you stop by The Busted Flush. You can't miss the place. Just get on James Street and walk toward all the noise. I'll be in there all night and I'll keep your mug full. It's the least I can do."

"Careful now. I just might take you up on that."

"Best be quick about it. If my wife hears I snuck back into town, this might be my last night as a free man for a good long while."

Ellis waved over his shoulder as he turned the gelding around and headed off down the street. As soon as the old man turned a corner, Clint heard someone else approaching from inside the stable. Coming out to meet him was a kid who looked to be about twelve or thirteen years old. He approached Eclipse and reached out to take the reins from Clint's hand.

"Looking for a place to put up your horse, mister?" the boy asked.

Clint nodded and removed a silver dollar from his pocket. "Will this be enough to take care of the next few days?"

"Sure."

Taking out an extra quarter, Clint flipped the coin into the boy's waiting palm and added, "That's yours for taking extra good care of him. Think you can do that?"

The boy's eyes widened and he nodded fiercely. "Yessir. I'll make sure he gets brushed every day and gets fed before any of the others."

Although the stable boy went on with his list of preferential treatment for Eclipse, Clint wasn't really listening. He was sure that the Darley Arabian was in good enough hands for now and wanted to get a room.

By the time he got checked into a hotel, Clint was ready to explore the local sight. The sun had dropped out of the sky completely, leaving nothing more than a smudge of dark

red and purple marking the place where it had been. With
the onset of night, Modillo seemed to truly come alive. Every
building down James Street was bright and teeming with life.
The sounds of raucous voices and player pianos spilled out
through doors propped open by crates or sleeping drunks to
mingle together in the middle of the street like invisible
dance partners.

Women dressed in next to nothing were already wandering
out to sit on the porches of cathouses to advertise their ser-
vices. Some leaned against the front doors while others sat
languidly on porch swings waiting for their next customer to
come walking by.

Mixed in with the bordellos were the saloons and gaming
parlors that ran the spectrum from dirty taverns the size of
shacks to lavish establishments complete with chandeliers
and gold-plated roulette wheels. The Busted Flush fell somewhere in between those two extremes. Although it was closer
in size to one of the chandelier places, it seemed to have
more in common with the shacks.

Not that The Busted Flush didn't appeal to Clint. On the
contrary, he found that the best saloons he'd been to had
their share of grit on the floors. If a place was too fancy, it
took away from the fun of gambling. Kind of like spending
too much time at a rich aunt's house; it just wasn't fun if
you had to worry about making a mess.

Clint walked inside The Busted Flush and stepped up to a
bar that was only about twice the length of a small sofa.
There was just enough room for a couple of beer taps and a
few bottles, which sat in front of a row of seven men
crowded together with their elbows resting on the chipped
cedar surface. Behind the bar was a rack of bottles that
looked like it was about to fall over when confronted by a
strong enough breeze. At one time there had obviously been
a mirror hung on the wall next to the rack, but all that remained now was a frame and a few large chunks of glass.

The walls sported so many bullet holes that Clint was surprised he couldn't hear the wind whistling through them.
Most of the space inside was taken up by two roulette wheels
and at least ten poker tables. Lined up along the farthest wall

was a row of faro tables that seemed to attract more action than anything else. Clint shook his head as he headed toward an empty chair at one of the poker tables. No matter how hard he tried, he couldn't figure out why anyone would buck the tiger at playing faro. The odds were so bad that it made more sense to just hand over your money to the dealers rather than go through the motions of actually playing.

The dealer at the table Clint had chosen was in the process of shuffling when he looked up to glance at the newest player.

"Mind if I sit in with you fellas?" Clint asked.

Shrugging, the dealer said, "Fifty-dollar minimum to buy in."

Clint fished out the money and handed it over. After receiving his chips, he anted up and waited for his cards. While the dealer finished shuffling the deck a few more times, Clint looked around the table to see who he would be playing with. "Pleased to meet you all," he said. "My name's Clint Adams."

The man sitting directly across from him nodded with obvious recognition, but didn't seem overly impressed. Just looking at his clothes, one might have thought he owned the saloon . . . as well as several other businesses in this part of town. His black shirt was made from a shiny silk that caught what little light there was in the place and tossed it around like a luminous plaything. Over that was a well-tailored pin-striped vest with the gold chain of a pocket watch crossing over the slight paunch of his belly. "I'm Matt Barstow," he said after giving Clint an offhanded wave.

To Clint's right was a lanky man who looked to be in his mid- to late-twenties. Dressed simply in a rumpled shirt that was stained beneath his arms and neck with perspiration, the man had a bushy mustache that all but covered his entire mouth. If the guy had chosen to breathe through his nose, his bottom lip would have been completely covered. Once Clint got a whiff of the odor floating off of the sweaty man, he realized why the previous occupant of his chair had left so early in the evening. The man seemed annoyed that Clint was looking at him for more than two seconds and showed it by attempting to growl menacingly. The grimace looked more like he was taking a painful squat in the outhouse.

Suppressing a chuckle, Barstow dismissed the sweaty figure with a shake of his head. "Don't mind him, Mister Adams. That's just Mike's way. He won't bite ya."

To Clint's left was a man of about the same age as the first, but in much better condition. This one's hair didn't stand up at odd angles and his clothes appeared to have been washed within the last week. His skin had the rich darkness of a native Mexican and the smoothness of a boy who had yet to see much beyond the limits of his hometown. He wore a plain blue shirt with a deputy's badge pinned to the chest. Seeing that Clint was looking in his direction, the deputy extended a hand. "The name's John Rivera. Pleased to meet you, Mister Adams. You wouldn't be . . ."

"Spit it out, Johnny," Barstow bellowed. "Ask him if he's *the* Clint Adams. I was just about to."

Clint leaned forward to accept the cards as they began coming at him from across the table. "Well, I don't know about all that, but I'm the only Clint Adams that I've heard of."

Barstow stared across the table into Clint's eyes. The longer he looked, the more tension seemed to settle over the table. It lasted until the final card was dealt and then Barstow picked up his hand. Collecting his cards without looking away from Clint, he let his smile drop for just a fraction of a second. The effect was similar to catching a fleeting glimpse of a rattlesnake during a thunderstorm. One minute there was only shadow and when the lightning flickered . . . there it was: gone just as quickly as it had appeared.

"Let's just see what this legend's made of," Barstow said with a sly wink.

FOUR

Surprisingly enough, even the man dressed in sweaty rags managed to call Barstow's first bet. Mike looked more than a little nervous, but Clint figured him for the type that would know better than to look scared at the table no matter how much it cost him. That would explain why the sweaty man couldn't afford to bathe.

The first thing Clint saw when he fanned his cards was a pair of deuces. Things looked up, however, once he saw the second five hiding behind the first. After discarding the four of clubs, he looked up to see how well the others at the table maintained their poker faces.

The young deputy on Clint's left was either an aspiring actor or was looking at a handful of nothing but garbage. On his other side, sweaty Mike was in the same position except was decidedly more pleased with what he'd been dealt. Then Clint looked across the table at Barstow and saw exactly what he'd expected: nothing.

Sitting with his head cocked to one side and his fingers drumming absently on the edge of the table, the well-dressed man wore his expression as if it had been painted onto his skull by an uninspired brush. His eyes held steady and stared down at his cards without so much as blinking more than once. Even when he sighed heavily, it was hard to say whether he was trying to act bored or was genuinely just taking in some air.

Clint watched as Barstow discarded a single card, and then turned his attention back to his own hand. Replacing the four he'd discarded was the three of clubs, which didn't do a damn thing for him. He looked down at the useless addition to his hand with the same amount of emotion he would have given a full house and waited for Barstow to start the next round of betting.

"That'll be another ten," Barstow said before flipping the appropriate chip on top of the rest.

Clint noted the way the man across from him rubbed his eyebrow and chin, but didn't think much of it until he saw how this hand turned out. Mike was the next one to bet and he was still grinning smugly. It was obvious to Clint, however, that that grin was plastered on through sheer force of will, which would lend him to believe that whatever the man had been hoping for hadn't come through.

"See yer ten," Mike grunted. "And raise two."

The chips clattered together as Mike added to the pile and sat back as though that alone was supposed to impress everyone.

Clint was fairly certain he had both his neighbors beaten. But rather than push his predictions and make a move too early, he shrugged noncommittally and counted out twelve dollars worth of chips. "I'll call."

The deputy shook his head in disappointment and glanced from his hand to his pile of chips and back again. To anyone paying attention, he might as well have been advertising the fact that he knew he should fold. "I'll . . . I guess I'll call."

Clint knew better than to write somebody off so quickly, but the deputy was too obvious to be anything but a bad card player. Even cheats tended to be more subtle than Rivera. If he was wrong, he knew he'd find out in less than a minute.

"Smart move," Barstow said as he laid down his cards. "Smart if you can beat tens and jacks, that is."

"Dammit," Mike spat as he tossed four spades and a diamond onto the table.

Clint set down his fives and twos right next to the deputy's pair of sevens.

Raking in the chips with a sweep of his hand, Barstow

glanced around at all the other players. "Looks like my luck held out after all. Maybe I'll be able to walk away without losing the shirt off my back this time."

When the next hand was dealt, the mood of the table had shifted to a quieter, more businesslike tone. The men kept their eyes down and their mouths shut. Even so, Clint was beginning to feel as though his relaxation had finally begun. Playing poker put him into a calm state of mind where nothing else existed beyond the confines of the table. The only problem he concerned himself with was winning the next hand and figuring out the other players' tells.

As the next few hands went along, Clint knew that Barstow's face seemed to itch whenever he had a decent hand. Mike swore under his breath when he wasn't dealt the right cards and swore even louder when he was. He was harder to read when he kept his mouth shut, though, mostly because he was such a terrible gambler. The sad truth was that better players were easier to read since there was more method to their actions. Amateurs tended to be more random in their decisions, which meant there was simply less to be read. That is, unless, they were scared.

And after only the first few hands, Clint knew that scared was the perfect word to describe Deputy Rivera. The young man wasn't about to start shaking or anything quite that drastic, but it was plain to see that he wasn't playing with money he could afford to lose. When he did win the occasional pot, his relief came in long, grateful breaths that kept him going to the next hand.

They'd been playing for about an hour when Clint was really starting to settle into the table's groove. He felt he'd gotten a fairly good read on his opponents with the possible exception of Barstow. He'd won enough to break even and he had the feeling that the best was yet to come.

Besides that, The Busted Flush was a saloon custom-made for gamblers. The lights were low and the music wasn't too loud. The waitresses paid attention to everyone's drinks and kept Clint's mug full without having to be reminded. One in particular paid special attention to Clint during one of his winning streaks and made sure to rub his shoulder every time she walked by.

The next hand opened for Clint with a pair of sevens and an ace, which something in the back of his mind told him to keep. He did and threw away the rest before looking around at the others. Mike was quiet for a change and Barstow never scratched until he got his second round of cards. Deputy Rivera didn't seem too nervous, which didn't bode well for Clint's measly pair.

It was his turn to open, so Clint tossed out a few chips. "I should know better, but I'll start with five."

Rivera nodded and threw in his chips. "Raise you two."

Barstow chuckled and flicked out twelve dollars. "Really shooting for the moon, huh deputy? Looks like the town fathers are paying you too much." With a practiced flip of his wrist, he tossed out another stack of chips. "See you and bump it up another ten. That's seventeen to you, Mike."

"Ah, what the hell. I'll call."

"Something wrong, Mike?" Barstow asked. "You look like you're about to sweat through your last good shirt. Oh wait a minute . . . you always look like that and you don't have any good shirts."

Even Clint had to laugh at that one as the whole table erupted into hysterics. The whole table except for Mike, that is. What struck Clint was the way the sweaty man chewed on his tongue as though it was dinner. His fists were clenched and he looked about ready to leap over the table with fists swinging. Mike was obviously a rough character, and did his best to intimidate rather than bluff the entire game.

But now, however, he seemed more whipped than anything else. Clint figured Barstow was an important man in town, but so far he hadn't displayed any aggression. When Mike dared to throw so much as an angry look in his direction, however, Barstow gave the man another peek at the snake lurking just beneath his surface. Everyone at the table caught a glimpse, but it was Mike who got the real look.

It was the first time that Mike seemed truly humbled. "You got me there, Mister Barstow," he said through clenched teeth.

"You're damned right I do. Now what'll it be?"

Mike threw down his cards and put his palms onto the table. "I fold."

By the time Barstow turned to look at Clint, the lightning had faded and the snake was back in hiding. "Then that's twelve to you, Adams."

Clint held the man's gaze without so much as blinking. He counted out his chips as though he held four sevens instead of only two. "Call."

When he got no reaction, Clint added a sly wink and a grin, which Barstow didn't like in the least.

The well-dressed man didn't make a big show of it, but the little twitch at the corner of his eye was more than enough to tell the tale. He wasn't used to people not backing down from him and when they did, he wasn't used to letting them get away with it.

Just for the hell of it, Clint raised another ten dollars before he even looked at the cards he got to replace the two he'd thrown away. Barstow didn't scratch and the deputy seemed confident enough to hang in there with the rest of them.

When the betting came around to him again, Barstow leaned back and gripped his cards tightly in one fist. The stack of money in front of him was healthy enough, but looked slightly smaller than Clint's. That fact obviously perturbed him as well when he surveyed the lay of the table.

"You gonna look at those cards, Mister Adams?" Barstow asked.

Clint gave an almost imperceptible shrug. "Would it make you feel better?"

"A man should always know what he's getting into before he charges straight ahead, don't you think?" Saying that, Barstow shot a quick glance over to Mike.

The sweaty thug leaned forward and looked over at Clint. Although he could feel the other man's eyes boring through him, Clint ignored everyone but Barstow. Right about then, the nagging little piece of his mind that had been uncomfortable at the thought of carrying around a broken pistol started to flare up. Clint could feel the modified Colt hanging from his hip, but knew that the best he could hope for if he fired it would be that it didn't blow up in his hand.

"I appreciate the concern," Clint said. "But I've seen more than enough."

Tossing in enough to cover the bet, Barstow muttered, "Suit yourself."

Clint placed his cards facedown over the two that had been dealt to him. After letting the table stew for a few seconds, he flipped over his hand to reveal his sevens as well as the pair of fours that he'd gotten on the second deal.

Just seeing the look on Barstow's face was enough to break Clint's calm facade. He smiled wide as he pulled in his winnings. "Would you look at that," Clint said. "Sometimes charging in does pay off."

FIVE

Shay Parkett had managed The Busted Flush since the saloon had been built. Although she only owned a quarter interest in the place, her entire life had been devoted to its upkeep ever since Matt Barstow had given her the job. She made sure the barkeeps didn't give away too many free drinks, and kept an eye on the dealers to make sure they didn't cheat any more than what was necessary.

Occasionally, some newcomer would make the mistake in thinking that she was one of the working girls patrolling the floor and would usually be limping for a good week afterward. But that didn't stop every man in the place from looking whenever she entered the room.

Standing at just over five and a half feet tall, the young woman dressed as though every night was reason enough to celebrate. On this night, she wore a white lacy gown with a feather boa draped over her shoulders. The front of the dress cut down low enough to give a generous view of her pert, rounded breasts. Her hips curved out just enough to accentuate her slender waist and when she walked, she knew damn well that she was the center of attention.

She kept her dark blonde hair cut just low enough to cover her neck and usually wore it pulled to one side. Having been at the saloon for several hours now, she was spending more time seated at one of the back tables rather than making her rounds between the games in progress. At the moment, she seemed particularly interested in the game involving Barstow and one of his hired thugs. They were playing against Deputy Rivera and some other man whom she'd never seen before.

Signaling with nothing more than a raised finger, she called over one of the dealers who'd been on his way to take over a faro table. Once the tall, muscular young man with the round spectacles made his way to her side, she leaned forward and pointed to Barstow's game.

"Do you know who that is, Marcus?"

The dealer looked over and nodded. "That's Mister Barstow and John Rivera."

"Not them. The one in between Rivera and Mike."

Marcus squinted for a few seconds through the lenses perched on the end of his nose and shook his head. "Never seen him before."

Shay watched silently for a few seconds as Barstow laid down his cards with that familiar smile on his face that she had quickly learned to hate. She covered her mouth to suppress the giggle that followed when she saw the stranger rake in the chips right out from under Barstow's seething frown.

"Before you start work, do me a favor," she said to the dealer. "Buy that man a drink and find out his name. Tell me what he says and . . . tell me what Mister Barstow says as well."

Shay watched as the dealer went over to the table and leaned down to talk to the man she'd been watching. Once he heard about the free drink, the man looked back to her table and tipped his hat. She pretended not to notice, even though she watched the stranger carefully out of the corner of her eye.

After the drink was delivered, the dealer went back one more time and spent a few minutes casually talking to the group of poker players. As soon as the next hand was dealt, Marcus excused himself and headed back across the room to report.

"Mister Barstow said you need to keep yourself in check until the game is good and over," the dealer recited. "He looked like he was about to throw that drink in my face as soon as he saw it wasn't meant for him."

Shay didn't even pretend to be concerned about that. "What about the stranger?" she asked. "Did you get his name?"

"He said he was Clint Adams."

"You say that like it should mean something to me. Has he been in here before? Does he have a tab the size of my arm or something?"

For a second, Marcus just stared at her as though he expected her to say that she was kidding. When all she did was look back at him, he leaned in closer and said in a hushed voice, "He's the Gunsmith."

"I thought Mister Peamont was the gunsmith in town."

"Don't you ever listen to the people that talk while they're in here? Clint Adams is a gunfighter. He's ridden with Bat Masterson and Bill Tilghman."

The way Shay nodded, it was unclear as to whether she really understood or was just trying to look as though she did. "I guess I've learned to stop listening when half the people that come through here start flapping their gums. What did Mister Adams say about the drink?"

" 'Thanks.' "

"Is that all?"

"If you were expecting more just tell me and I'll make some up. Now is there anything else you want me to do or can I get to work?"

She waved Marcus on and turned her head to get another look at the man who she now knew to be a famous gunfighter. Just thinking about meeting someone with that sort of reputation sent chills down Shay's spine. Suddenly her dress felt constricting and uncomfortable and she wanted to be out of it as soon as possible. More than that, she wanted him to take her out of it.

Just then she realized that the gunfighter was staring back at her and Shay turned to look in another direction. When she looked back at the poker game, she saw that Adams had turned his attention to his cards. Barstow was shooting angry looks toward Mike Tavitz, and Deputy Rivera looked as though he wished he was anyplace besides where he was.

Sometimes Shay felt sorry for that deputy. She'd even persuaded Barstow to raise the lawman's salary, but that didn't seem to ease poor Rivera's nerves. All it did was put the town's authority that much deeper into Barstow's pockets.

In fact, Clint Adams was the only man at that table who wasn't on Barstow's payroll. More than anything, she wished she could go over and sit down next to the gunfighter just to see what it was like when Barstow was put in his place.

Usually, once a newcomer found out who Barstow was or got an idea of the power he held, they went out of their way to please the man or get out of his sight. But Clint Adams had been sitting at that table for some time without so much as leaving to stretch his legs. And more than that . . . he was winning.

Yes, this man interested her very much. Rather than introduce herself right away, however, she decided to put it off until later that night. That way, she figured on getting the whole story of what had happened during his game with the most powerful man in Modillo.

SIX

It was getting close to midnight before Tannen and his boys rode back into Modillo. They'd spent the entire day on the move and nearly drove their animals into the ground taking the trail so fast with only a few minutes' rest in Split Creek while the horses caught their breath. All the while, Tannen had been chewing on the day's events in the back of his mind.

None of the cowboys were stupid enough to bring up the meeting they'd had with Ellis and the man who'd pulled his fat out of the fire. Although Tannen hadn't been planning on killing the old man, he figured on walking away with the coot's new gelding as well as whatever money was in his pockets. Losing that simple score was a blow to Tannen's pride. It stabbed at the pit of his stomach and made his trigger finger itch in anticipation of meeting up with those two one more time.

By the time he'd made it back to town, Tannen was just tired enough to put his payback off until the next day. He knew where the old man would be and he figured the other one wouldn't be far behind. For the moment, however, he needed to get off his horse and onto one of the girls from James Street.

As they rode into town, one of Tannen's cowboys came up from the back of the group until he was side by side with his leader. They were taking their time heading through the part of Modillo that went to sleep after the sun went down, although they could plainly hear the part of town that picked that particular time to wake up.

"What is it, Bart?" Tannen asked after the other man had come up beside him.

Bart had been riding with Tannen longer than anyone else in the crew and was given the most leeway when it came to speaking plainly regarding business matters. "What do you think Barstow will say?"

"Say about what? If you think he'll give a rat's ass about us not giving old Ellis a hard time, you'd be mistaken. That codger is just good for pocket money, you know that."

"Maybe that ain't what I was talking about."

"Then why don't you fill me in?"

Glancing back to make sure none of the other boys were close enough to hear, Bart looked over his shoulder and then leaned toward Tannen just to be sure. "What do you think he'll say when he hears that we all got rousted by one man? Mister Barstow is particular about appearances and that don't make us look so—"

Bart's words caught in his throat as Tannen's hand wrapped tightly around his neck. In less than a second, he could feel his face getting hot and pressure building up beneath his skin as though his skull was about to pop. Bright spots danced in front of Bart's eyes and the world seemed to be spinning in the wrong direction.

Tannen pulled the other man forward until his fist was the only thing keeping Bart from falling out of his saddle. He could also feel the blood pumping through his veins, but not from lack of air. Instead, it was rage that caused his senses to skew inside his brain and his heart to slam against the inside of his ribs.

"We been together a long time," Tannen hissed. "That's why I'm talkin' to you right now instead of putting my gun to your head and pulling the trigger. Before you turn blue, tell me if you really think I got rousted by that one man."

Bart knew the answer that he wanted to say. Unfortunately, it wasn't the same answer that would have allowed him to draw in a clean breath. He could feel his muscles starting to relax and his body slump forward, which put him precariously close to the edge of his horse.

"I . . . I didn't mean . . ."

"Better save your breath and pick your words carefully, Bart. I can feel the life draining out of ya. Now it wasn't a hard question. Do you think I was really rousted by one man . . . yes or no?"

". . . N-no . . ."

"There," Tannen said while easing up on his grip around the other man's throat. "You're not so stupid after all."

With a little nudge, Tannen shoved the other man away just hard enough to throw him back into the saddle. Bart hacked loudly a few times and spat onto the ground. Realizing that the rest of the boys were watching, he straightened up and acted as though every vein in his neck didn't feel as though it had been crushed.

"What I was going to say," Bart continued with a little more respect in his voice, "is that Ellis is surely going to go back to town and tell everyone what happened." When he saw the fire blazing behind Tannen's eyes, he added, "Or he'll tell everyone a story about what happened. Either way, he won't make us look good. You know how Mister Barstow gets. Once he hears them lies, he'll be after us. What should we tell him?"

The group of riders had stopped on the edge of the gambling district where they could just make out the sounds of every sin imaginable being committed within one square block. The men lined up behind Tannen and Bart were anxious to move on, but not so anxious that they were willing to risk their own necks.

Tannen sat perched in his saddle, looking out at the end of James Street like a general getting ready to invade. He looked over to Bart and then back to the remaining men. "If Barstow asks, we'll tell him that we caught up with that cocky son of a bitch and put him down like a dog."

Bart seemed hesitant to say anything else, but forced himself to do so anyhow. "But that ain't the truth. Hell, Tannen, that fella's probably here in town right now."

Turning back to look down the street, Tannen grabbed

hold of his reins and bared his crooked dirty teeth in a vicious smile. "Then let's start askin' around until we find that bastard and then drag him out in the street so's we can put some lead into him. That way it won't be a lie at all."

Bart, along with all the other cowboys, smiled. Up until now, they'd been starting to have their doubts about the man they took their orders from. Now that the old Tannen had returned, they were more than happy to follow.

All at once, the six riders took off down James Street in search of their prize.

SEVEN

If Clint's faith ever started to falter, it was always restored at the poker table. Although the tide had turned several times in the hours he'd been in his chair, the pile of chips in front of him had remained fairly consistent. He knew that cheating was so common that it was damn near expected whenever any amount of money was involved. Only truly talented players could make a living on cards without knowing several good tricks. And while Clint didn't make his living from gambling, he held his own without once resorting to trickery.

Nights like this one, he knew, were his reward.

As he sat and watched a thug like Mike Tavitz lose nearly everything he had and then palm his way back to a small profit, Clint managed to beat him by using skill, brains and no small amount of luck. Those things had also kept him alive during Barstow's streaks, which had threatened to wipe out everyone at the table. For rich men like Barstow, cheating wasn't necessary. They had enough money to outlast all comers.

Clint looked over to the deputy, who somehow had managed to hold on to a few lonely chips. Rivera was sweating bullets as he discarded one card and waited for its replacement.

"You going to be all right?" Clint asked the deputy.

Rivera wiped his brow with the back of his hand and nodded solemnly. "Sure, Mister Adams. But this might just do me in."

Clint was looking at kings and fives on the deal and when he discarded a stray nine, he turned back to Rivera. "Well I hope you're not gambling away your life savings, because I'm feeling lucky."

Barstow hated it when other players besides himself talked it up like that and Clint knew it. That was the only reason he said such things at all. Normally, Clint liked to keep quiet and concentrate on his game, but getting under Barstow's skin had become part of the night's entertainment and was more than worth the effort.

The well-dressed man tapped his fingers on the edge of the table and shook his head like a disapproving father. "You gonna talk or are you gonna play?"

"I am going to play," Clint said as he looked at his newest card. The jack of diamonds was no help to him whatsoever, but he still thought he might be able to bluff his way through to victory.

Just then, Clint noticed Barstow's hand sneak beneath the bottom of his vest and flick back out again. When he brought that hand back up and slipped in the card he'd plucked from his private stash, Barstow moved with a catlike grace that Clint would have admired if he hadn't spotted it so early in the evening.

One thing that he'd learned from playing cards with Doc Holliday was that a good poker player didn't need to cheat. He did, however, need to spot those that did. Once you picked them out, it was just a matter of out-classing them. Clint knew his chances of winning this hand based on his cards alone would have been good in a straight game. But when one of the players was cheating, that cast a whole new light on his odds.

The next round of betting started off slow. A small raise here, another couple of dollars there. Eventually, Barstow couldn't hold his water any longer and he began tossing in ten extra dollars per shot.

Looking over the others, Clint saw that Mike was about to crawl out of his skin. Every time it came to him, he looked

over to Barstow and when Barstow didn't look back, the
sweaty man grudgingly bumped up the bet by a dollar or
two. Finally, Barstow gave him an annoyed nod.

"I got no business in this anymore," Mike said as he threw
his cards onto the table. "I fold. Hope you folks choke on
them chips you won from me. At least I got enough to buy
a few more drinks." And with that, he took his last dollar
and walked over to the bar.

"Guess that just leaves us three," Clint said. "Refresh my
memory . . . what's the bet up to?"

Barstow spoke in a gravelly baritone that reflected every
one of the five hours they'd been playing. "Twenty more to
stay in the game."

There was some kind of commotion going on near the
front door as the sound of scuffling and angry voices made
its way back to Clint's table. He turned to look, but couldn't
see much through the other men who'd gotten up to watch
what appeared to be a fistfight.

"Never mind that, Adams," Barstow said. "Just put yer
money or your cards on the table."

Clint could feel Barstow's irritability growing with every
second that passed. Staring at his cards although he'd already
memorized every line on their surface, Clint nurtured the
other man's frustration as though it was a fine wine. The
longer he let it sit and grow, the sweeter it became.

Another thing he'd learned from Doc was that emotions
had no place at the card table. Emotional men lost their per-
spective along with their edge. Emotions caused more emotions and in turn brought on mistakes. Since it was obvious
Clint couldn't win a game where his opponent padded his
own hand, he would force Barstow to slip up. Judging by
the tension crackling around the rich man like desert lightning, it wouldn't be too much longer before that mistake was
made.

After a few more loaded seconds ticked by, Clint lifted his
head to look directly into Barstow's eyes. The stare was different than the ones he'd used to size up the table. This one
locked onto Barstow like a hawk, causing the well-dressed
man to freeze in place.

"Tell you what, Barstow," Clint said gravely. "I'll push over all my chips right now and slide them right into that tall stack of yours if you can do me one little favor."

For the most fleeting of instants, something flashed across Barstow's face that seemed oddly out of place on a man with his severe, chiseled features: fear. "What favor is that?"

"Stand up and open your vest."

"What?"

"I'd just like to know how many more face cards you've got stashed in that pocket you've been dipping into for the last two hours."

"If you're making an accusation, I hope you're ready to back it up."

The commotion near the front door spilled inside the saloon and got close enough for Clint to recognize a familiar voice.

Laying down his cards, Clint showed his pair of kings and pair of fives. "Now I'm no fortune-teller, but I'll just bet you started this hand with a pair, seeing as how you discarded three cards. Now, with the card you took from that inside pocket, I'll bet you've got three-of-a-kind, which would be just enough to show me up."

Barstow didn't even try to hide the dangerous look in his eyes. Before, the man's true self showed itself in glimpses. Now the light shone on the snake's face with all the force of the sun. When he slammed his cards onto the table, Barstow's fist shook over the jack of clubs, queen of spades and the three sixes as if he was about to smash them through the polished wood.

Clint smiled back at him. "Now, I know I'm not a mind reader. So that must make me either right about you cheating or real lucky."

"No, Mister Adams. I'd say you're anything but lucky."

The entire saloon had gotten suddenly quiet, which made it easy for Clint to pick out the thump of footsteps approaching him from behind. They stopped about five feet short of the table, and threw the room into complete silence.

"Excuse me," came a voice that, although it was meek, still dropped like a hammer through the dead air.

Barstow's eyes flicked over to the one who'd spoken and seemed surprised when he saw that Deputy Rivera was still at the table.

"If all this is about the cards you're holding," Rivera said, "then maybe I can put an end to your dispute."

Without waiting for either man to say another word, Rivera put his own cards on the table. They were the ten and jack of hearts, the queen of clubs and the king and ace of diamonds. Looking down at the straight, Barstow's jaw dropped so low that it nearly bounced off the table. When Clint got a look at the winning hand, he leaned back in his chair and started to laugh.

"That," Barstow said as he pushed away from the table and got to his feet, "is about enough of this bullshit." His hand flashed toward the pistol hanging at his side just as he motioned for the men behind Clint to step in closer. "This is my place and you live by *my* rules! It's either that." He seethed while taking the gun from its holster. "Or you can die by them."

EIGHT

As soon as Barstow went for his gun, the entire saloon erupted into chaos. Clint could hear the footsteps closing in behind him as though they were the only noise in the room. He'd been leaning back when the action started and then leaned a little farther while taking a quick look over his shoulder. Just as he'd figured, the man he'd chased off outside of town was coming up behind him with a gun clutched in one hand. Things might have gotten crazy in the space of a second, but Clint had been waiting for the man with the rotten teeth to track him down all night.

Teetering on the brink of falling over backward, Clint balanced on his chair while reaching back with his right hand. Tannen had been about to put his gun to Clint's back when Clint made his move. Tannen's first impulse was to twist his gun out of the way before it got knocked from his hand.

Clint had hoped the man would do just that and when his hand closed around the pistol, all he needed to do was turn his wrist and continue the motion the other man had started. Tannen howled with pain and let go of the gun as though it had suddenly become red-hot as his hand nearly snapped from being turned in the wrong direction.

Once he had Tannen's gun in hand, Clint shifted his weight forward and pushed himself toward the table. He could see Barstow's hand moving up to point a pistol at Deputy Rivera's head. Before it could get there, Clint's momentum had pushed his body up far enough to set his chair on all four legs again, continuing on until he was now tipping forward.

With his left hand, Clint reached out to snatch the gun away from Barstow just as the rich man pulled the trigger. Clint tightened his grip around the weapon, putting the base of his thumb beneath the hammer so that the firing pin lodged into his flesh rather than set off a round into the deputy's face.

By the time the blood started trickling down Clint's hand, he pushed the chair back and was on his feet. Clint clenched his teeth and pushed back with his thumb, digging the pin farther into his skin until the hammer clicked back into place. With a quick motion, he tossed the gun up and moved his hand around so that he was holding it by the grip. Clint pointed each of the guns he'd taken back at their owners and stood so that he was positioned directly between both men.

"All right now," Clint said calmly. "Let's just stop and think about this before things get too far out of hand."

Although he knew better than to hope that any of the men would actually take his advice, Clint used the next few seconds to assess the situation. All in all, it was far from good.

It looked as though several men at some of the other tables were getting up to stand behind Barstow. Tannen had brought in two of his own, and Clint could only assume that the rest wouldn't be far behind.

He then looked over to Deputy Rivera. The young man seemed rooted to his chair. Although he wore a gun, he made no move to pull it.

"You can get up now," Clint said to the deputy. "You witnessed everything that went on. Now how about you settle this nice and legally before someone gets hurt?"

Rivera got to his feet and looked as though he was about to say something. But before a word came out of his mouth, he looked toward Barstow with the same deference as Mike had done when looking for his boss's approval. It was at that moment that Clint realized just who the deputy took his orders from. A cold feeling worked its way through Clint's bones and the bottom dropped out of his stomach.

He was on his own.

His face twisting up with a wicked grin, Barstow held his hand out toward Rivera. "Give me your gun, deputy," he said.

As soon as she'd seen Tannen and two of his men storm through the front door, Shay ran behind the bar and went for the shotgun that she kept there whenever fights got too far out of hand. By the time she poked her head back up, she could see that there were several other men in the back of the room stepping forward with their hands on their guns and murderous intent written across their faces.

She'd seen that look plenty of times to know the difference between a brewing bar fight and the beginnings of a shooting. In the middle of it all, positioned between both approaching groups, was the stranger who she'd been watching for most of the evening. At first, Shay had been worried that the bullets would start to fly before she could even try to calm things down. But then, in the space it took for her to get truly worried, Clint had burst into motion and had disarmed the two men closest to him.

Her heart beat wildly inside her chest and the blood raced through her veins. She was scared, but not too scared that she couldn't appreciate just how fast that famous gunfighter had moved. Suddenly, the situation didn't seem quite as bad.

Turning to the bartender who had put his back against the rack of half-empty bottles, she stood up straight and whispered, "See if you can get outside and keep any more of Tannen's boys from getting in here."

The barkeep looked at her as though she'd just told him to perch on top of the bar and flap his arms. "Are you crazy? That fella's well past anything we could do for him. Besides, Barstow would—"

"Do you have your gun on you?"

"Yes, but—"

"Then step outside and don't pull it until you get there. With everyone watching this, nobody will probably even notice what you're doing. I figure that man's odds are bad enough without them getting any worse."

Although the barkeep didn't seem too pleased about it, he knew better than to argue with Shay Parkett . . . especially when she had a shotgun in her hands. He sidestepped behind the bar and eased through the crowd. He got a lot of warning glances, but nobody made a move to stop him, and when he got outside, the barkeep felt as though he'd managed to slip right between the fingers of the reaper himself.

Once she saw that the barkeep was out the front door, Shay took a deep breath, held it for a second and let it out. It helped to clear her head a bit but didn't make her feel any better about what she was preparing to do.

Before she had a chance to step out from behind the bar, Shay threw herself back down behind it as one of the men standing next to Tannen drew his gun and pointed it at the poker table. As soon as the first move was made, everything else went straight to hell and The Busted Flush became a powder keg.

NINE

Clint was about to warn Deputy Rivera not to hand over his gun when he spotted a movement out of the corner of his eye. He turned to get a look at what was happening and caught a glimpse of light flickering off the dull metal of a gun's barrel. Before he could think, Clint's reflexes set his body into motion and he dropped straight down into a crouch.

Barstow yelled something when he saw the gun pointing in his direction and immediately dropped to the floor like a sack of grain. Once there, he glared across at Clint and gave him another one of his wicked smiles.

"You ain't getting out of here alive, Adams," Barstow said. "I don't care how good you are."

Looking up, Clint saw that Rivera had his gun out and was about to hand it down to Barstow. Before the deputy was able to pass the weapon off, Clint put his shoulder beneath the edge of the table and pushed up with his legs until the entire thing tipped over onto its side, pinning Rivera to the floor beneath it.

As soon as the gun fell from the deputy's hand and clattered to the floor, Clint swept it away with his boot. Keeping low to the floor, Clint then turned around to face Tannen and his men, making sure to keep his back to the overturned table for what little cover it would provide. He then snapped back the hammers of both the guns he was holding and readied them to fire.

The one who'd drawn first kept himself from pulling the trigger until he had a clear shot. Now that Clint had him in sight, the gunman lowered his aim and thumbed the hammer back.

Clint dropped to one side just as the other man's gun went off and blew a hole through the table. Splinters rained down on Clint's side like a wooden drizzle as he rolled to his left and came to rest beneath the neighboring table. Resting on his heels, Clint coiled his body like a spring. He could hear people in the bar running in every possible direction. The ones that had been coming up behind Barstow were now closing in on him in an attempt to trap him between themselves and Tannen's crew.

Another shot blasted through the air and punched a hole through the table less than a foot away from Clint's head. Waiting until the last second, Clint pushed up with his legs until he felt his shoulder blades slam against the bottom of the table. When he rose to his full height, the table flew behind him and leveled the men that had been trying to come up behind him.

Clint's back was burning with the pain caused from the table, but it only served to make him that much more focused on what he was doing. The first thing he saw after standing up was Tannen's gunman lining up his third shot. Before the other man could even think too long about pulling the trigger, Clint had drawn a bead and squeezed the trigger of the pistol clenched in his left fist.

One moment the gunman was getting ready to fire off another round, and the next, a chunk of hot lead tore through his skull and chewed a tunnel all the way out the other side. His finger clenched around the trigger, sending a wild shot into the air well above Clint's head as his body pitched backward as though it had been kicked by a mule.

Clint saw Tannen moving for his own weapon and took aim with the pistol in his right hand. Before he could fire, however, the third cowboy lunged forward to grab hold of Clint's arm just above the wrist. Looking over to the man's

face, Clint saw it was the one whose gun he'd taken as all
of this had began. Not one to steal property that didn't belong
to him, Clint gladly returned the pistol . . . butt first and right
between the cowboy's eyes.

Teetering back on suddenly unsteady feet, the cowboy
shook his head and reached up to touch his brow. There was
already a generous flow of blood coursing over his face and
when he felt the warm fluid between his fingers, his eyes
started to glaze over and he fell backward onto the floor.

"That's two down," Clint said as he started walking toward
Tannen. "Care to make it three?"

Suddenly, the entire room seemed to be closing in on Clint
from all sides. On an instinctual level, he felt like an animal
caught in a trap. Unfortunately, every other part of his brain
told him that that was exactly what he was.

While most of the people inside the saloon had cleared
out, there were still about ten left. Some were helping Barstow get to his feet and lifting the table off of Deputy Rivera.
The rest were making their way toward Clint. Although they
seemed unsure about pulling their weapons, they didn't look
ready to back off, either.

Scanning their faces, Clint saw that most of them were
more scared than anything else. They seemed concerned
about Barstow, but only so far as keeping the other man
healthy. When they looked toward Clint, they turned their
eyes away and shuffled on their feet, unsure if they even
wanted to attract his attention.

Tannen, on the other hand, was another story. He glared
at Clint with enough fury in his eyes to start a fire. His hand
shook over his gun and his teeth ground together spitefully.

"You better listen to that shred of common sense telling
you to keep away from that gun," Clint said. "This is just a
poker game gone wrong. One man died because he was stupid." Turning toward the crowd near Barstow, Clint raised
his voice and added, "You all hear me? I'm not about to
shoot anyone else as long as nobody does anything they
shouldn't."

When he saw that no one was about to make a move
toward him just yet, Clint stepped up to Tannen and looked

him dead in the eye. For a second, both men stood still and
waited for the other to jump. When neither did, Clint began
moving toward the door.

"What the hell are you waiting for?" came Barstow's en-
raged voice. "Kill that son of a bitch!"

Clint spun around to find Tannen right behind him. But
he wasn't drawing down on Clint. In fact, Tannen was diving
to the side.

It was then that Clint looked closer to where Barstow was
standing. Next to him was the sweat-stained Mike, who must
have finally found his way through the crowd and to his
boss's side. Clint could still hear Barstow's words echoing
through the room when he saw Mike's hand flashing toward
his gun.

With a single motion of his arm and body turning at once,
Clint brought up his gun and took aim before Mike was able
to cock his hammer back. By the time Mike's gun was ready
to fire, the weapon in Clint's fist barked once and spit its
bullet through a cloud of smoke.

The round caught Mike in the chest and knocked him back
half a step. But his body was still trying to carry out Barstow's command and he managed to keep his gun trained on
Clint.

Used to his own modified Colt, Clint nearly tried to take
another shot without pulling back the hammer. But preparing
the borrowed gun would have cost him the last second of his
life, so he instead raised his other hand and fired the second
pistol. That bullet struck a little low, punching a dark hole
in Mike's solar plexus and doubling him over with a pained
grunt.

The gun in Mike's hand went off, but not until the arm
holding it had fallen like a limp rag at his side, sending a
bullet into the planks near his feet. Mike stayed upright for
a second or two as though he was being held up by a string.
Finally, he let out a shuddering breath and he fell onto his
back.

"He killed Mike," one of the other men near Barstow said
in a voice full of disbelief. Rushing over to Mike's twitching
body, the man looked down and then back at everyone gath-

ered around. In a louder, more forceful voice, he said, "That bastard killed Mike!"

Clint had managed to clear a path to the front door and was almost outside when the saloon once again erupted. Although most of the men were headed for the back door, a few picked up chairs, guns or whatever they could get their hands on and started rushing toward Clint.

And just before a group of half-drunk gamblers swarmed past him, Barstow locked eyes with Clint one more time. For a split second, they weren't in the middle of a fight or standing on floorboards soaked with blood. For that instant, they were still looking at one another as opponents.

Clint had made his moves and did the best with what he had, but just like before, the deck was stacked against him. Barstow knew it and savored the feeling of gaining the upper hand. He wore that same smirk, made sure Clint was aware of what was coming . . . and winked.

"Full house beats your pair," Barstow said.

TEN

A single blast thundered through the saloon that shook the glasses on the bar and caused every soul in the place to freeze in their tracks.

"That's enough!" came a voice that was almost as forceful as the shotgun's eruption. "Anyone else makes a move toward that man and they'll have to answer to me."

Shay had seen more than she could take. Although she'd been in the saloon business for more than six years and had seen her share of violence, she'd never seen as much blood as she had today. When the shooting had started, it was all she could do to get down and stay there as the bullets flew and the bodies hit the floor.

But once she'd gotten used to the situation as much as she could, she crawled out from around the bar and watched as Barstow and his men did their best to trap another human being like a rat and gun him down in cold blood. She watched as the stranger had tried to get away and shoot only when he had to. But no matter how many chances he gave them, the others seemed determined to kill him.

Finally, after Mike made his play and lost, Shay could tell that Barstow would say whatever he could to get his men to fire until that stranger was dead. Something inside of her snapped at that moment. It caused her to get to her feet, grip the shotgun tightly in both hands and give the stranger a chance to live.

At first, she tried saying something that would catch everyone's attention. All that she could get out of her mouth was some vague arrangement of syllables that nobody inside the saloon could even hear. Then she figured on catching people's attention by setting the gun off. As soon as her finger found the trigger, the gun practically exploded in her gasp, scaring herself twice as much as it scared anybody else inside The Busted Flush.

But at least she had everyone's attention. After that, the words had flowed out of her rather easily.

Shay saw that several men inside the place actually moved to obey her command. Even though she was holding a shotgun, she still thought that there wouldn't be anybody that would actually listen to her. It took a great deal of work to erase the pleased smile off of her face and to keep her stern expression solidly in place.

"That's better," she said once the men who'd been rushing toward the stranger actually backed off and headed in the opposite direction. "Now you let him leave here and then you keep away from him once he's outside."

Without planning on it, Shay had moved herself so that she stood between the stranger and Tannen. After she heard the front door open and close, she turned quickly to make sure that he was gone and then looked back to the unhappy faces glaring at her with the promise of violence.

Suddenly, all the fear that she'd been expecting to feel the entire time came rushing back into Shay's body until her palms grew hot and wet where they were wrapped around the shotgun.

Even though she tried to fight them back, the shakes were too powerful and they claimed her body slowly but surely. As she made her way to the front door, she could feel first her legs beginning to quiver and then her hands starting to tremble. It didn't help matters when she saw that the gunmen were still moving toward her just waiting for the right moment to make their move and overtake her by force.

"Don't be foolish, Shay," came a voice from the middle of the room, which, although it was trying to sound calm and reassuring, made her feel cold and threatened.

The voice belonged to Barstow, who stepped out from the small crowd with both hands held out in front of him. "You must've seen how this all started," he said. "Therefore you know that it was him who drew first blood."

"Maybe so," Shay said once she had one foot out the door, "but I've known you and your men for too long. I'll bet he had every right to be upset with you. It's never enough for you to just beat someone. You've got to humiliate them as well. And if you can't figure out a way to humiliate them, you know plenty of ways to hurt them."

"Why, whatever do you mean?"

"He may have drawn first blood, but I'm sure you more than asked for it."

Barstow took another couple of steps forward until he all but ran into the end of Shay's shotgun barrel. He seemed unconcerned with the weapon and was already straining to get a look past her. That show of arrogance only infuriated Shay more and she jabbed the barrel into Barstow's chest.

"You still think you can't be killed?" Shay asked once Barstow finally looked into her eyes.

Seeing that he didn't have any choice but to talk to the woman, Barstow looked at her over the shotgun as if the weapon wasn't even there. "Sure I can be killed. Just not by you. I'm a good judge of character, darlin', and I've known you for a long time. You've always had spirit. I just couldn't say where this came from all of a sudden."

"Maybe this has been brewing a long time and you were too busy trying to run the town from this saloon to notice."

"Actually, I've been doing a damn good job of running this town from here."

"That would explain why Modillo has become such a rat-infested stopover for every mangy cowboy who can get his hands on a gun."

Shay took another quick look outside and saw the barkeep waving frantically at her. She couldn't see a trace of the stranger. "If you don't mind, I'd like to get the hell out of here before you send one of your killers after me since I dared to raise my voice against the high and mighty Matthew Barstow."

Stepping up next to his boss, Tannen began walking toward her as though he knew the order to do so would be
coming any second. As soon as he did, however, Barstow
stopped him with a restraining arm.

"Let her go," Barstow said. "She's just upset, that's all."
To Shay, he added, "You go home and rest. This has been
a hard night for all of us."

Shay had plenty more that she wanted to say to the well-
dressed boss, but instead she backed out through the door
and made sure it was closed all the way before turning her
back on the place. The barkeep waited for her with a small
revolver clenched in a shaky hand.

"What were you saying to Barstow?" he asked. "It
sounded like you were trying to pick a fight with the man."

Looking around for any sight of the stranger, she took a
moment to let her eyes adjust to the pitch darkness outside
the saloon. "I was just trying to buy some time for that poker
player."

"You mean Clint Adams?"

"That's the one. Which way did he go?"

"This way."

The answer didn't come from the barkeep, but rather from
the alley between The Busted Flush and the next building
over. When Shay looked toward the sound, she saw Clint
step out from the shadows.

"When Barstow comes out, tell him I went the other direction," she said without taking her eyes from the shadowy
figure at the foot of the alley. "And if you don't see me for
a while, don't worry. I'll be in good hands."

ELEVEN

Clint stood in the alley and waited until he knew for sure that the woman was on her way. She was still clutching the shotgun in her hands when she turned and started heading in his direction.

"I don't think you need that anymore," he said as she ran into the alley with the weapon held in front of her.

For a second, Shay didn't know what he was talking about. Then she looked down and nearly threw the shotgun away. Instead, she lowered it so that it pointed toward the ground. "Sorry. I guess I was just caught up in the moment."

Motioning for her to follow, Clint walked through the alley and came out behind the buildings lining James Street. He stopped for a second and listened for any indication that the men from The Busted Flush were trying to follow. All he could hear was a woman singing inside the building next door to the saloon and several drunkards doing their best to accompany her. As far as he could tell, the street and alley were clear.

Clint held out his hand. "Thanks for helping me back there. I really appreciate it."

Shay took his hand and shook it enthusiastically. "I've been waiting for an excuse to point a gun at Matt Barstow for a long time now. Actually, I should probably thank you for giving me the opportunity."

The skin of her hand was warm and a little tough. She

47

seemed to be more excited than scared, but Clint still got the idea that she wasn't used to being in situations where she was on the wrong end of a gun. Her breaths were hard and steady as though she'd run an entire block instead of the few feet between front door and alley.

"My name's Clint."

"I know. I've heard of you."

"Well, most people have."

"Don't get too much of a swelled head. I only heard that name a few hours ago when you first sat down to play in my bar."

Blushing, Clint looked away and suppressed a laugh at his own expense. "Did you hear anything else about me?"

She held his gaze for a second or two and let a promising smile cross her lips. "Just that you were some kind of famous gunman. I kind of had you figured for one of those men that comes through here and likes to impress the ladies with a tall tale about how he rode with William Bonney or robbed the Union Pacific."

"You see a lot of gunmen, huh?"

"No. Just a lot of bullshit artists. Most of them would've dropped to their knees and kissed Barstow's feet after what happened in there. But not you." Her eyes drifted over Clint's body and her smile widened just a little bit. "That's why I did what I did. After all, who do you think's going to have to clean up the bodies you left behind?"

Clint was leaning against the wall, listening to what the blonde had to say. As much as he hated to admit it, he didn't like being forced to leave that saloon. Even though he still had those two guns stuck in his belt, he wasn't so familiar with them that he would take on a room full of shooters. The modified Colt had seen him through plenty of rough times and he'd worked on it so that just having that gun would give him an edge over odds even as bad as the ones he'd just escaped. He still had the New Line on him, but it had never come into play.

The smart thing to do was to get out of there before yet another thing happened to throw him off balance. There were too many in that place and only one of them needed to get in one lucky shot. If they didn't get him, Clint would have been forced to get them, which would have meant a whole lot of unnecessary death.

Getting out of that saloon made sense, but that didn't mean he had to like it.

"You want to go back in there, don't you?" the blonde asked.

Clint shook himself out of his thoughts and noticed the way she was still looking at him. "I never did catch your name."

"It's Shay Parkett."

"Is Shay short for something?"

"Cheyenne. Folks around here don't treat Indians too well and it makes things a lot smoother for me if I just go by Shay. My daddy used to call me that when I was little."

"That's a pretty name . . . both of them. And before you ask again, yes, I do want to go back in there. Just another bit of evidence that pride isn't linked to common sense."

Shay looked quickly down the alley and hefted the shotgun over her shoulder. "We'd best get going, then."

"Answer a question for me?"

"I'll try."

"Why'd you really help me back there? From what I could see, Barstow is a powerful man. He's got the law and the killers in this town working for him. He owns that saloon, which means he's your boss as well. Why go against him like that?"

Looking down for a second, Shay took a deep breath as though she was trying to fight back oncoming tears. When she looked up again, the smile was gone from her face, making Clint sorry he'd ever asked that question.

"Honestly . . . I don't know why I helped you. Barstow's cheated more men at cards than I can count. And he's stood by to watch others get killed more times than that. But you were beating him at his own game even after he started cheating. I've never seen that before.

"And when the shooting started, you nearly beat him there, too. I ain't even heard of that happening before." Shay put a hand on her hip and tilted her head as she looked at Clint.

There were hints of the smile returning, but it wasn't quite there yet. "I helped you because you seemed special, Clint Adams. And you weren't about to leave that place until you got shot or killed."

"I guess I'm not too good at backing away from a fight once I've been thrown into one."

There were still no unusual sounds coming from the saloon, which told Clint that Barstow and his men had chosen to back off for now. He reached out and put an arm over Shay's shoulders so he could pull her in close to his side. She fit perfectly against his body. Her hips were easy, sloping curves that twitched back and forth invitingly when she walked. After moving the shotgun to her opposite hand, she slid an arm around Clint's waist.

They walked behind the buildings until they were almost to the end of the row before ducking into an alley and taking that back to James Street. Once they were there, they headed away from the saloon district and back toward Clint's hotel.

"You're shaking," he said.

"Just thinking about what happened. Actually, I'm more worried about what's going to happen."

"You mean Barstow?"

"He'll be after you."

"What about the sheriff? I know the deputy is with Barstow, but does that mean all the town's law is, too?"

"There isn't any law. Rivera wears that badge as more of a decoration than anything else. Now that he lost hold of you tonight, Barstow will be out for blood and believe me . . . he won't care much whose blood he gets."

Clint reflexively looked over his shoulder, keeping a sharp eye on every dark window and all the shadowy doorways. Seeing as how it was well past midnight and the moon was nothing more than a sliver of white hanging in the sky, there were plenty of windows and doorways to be watched. The effort alone was enough to wear Clint out. But that, combined with everything else that had happened, exhausted him right down to the bone.

"Do you have somewhere safe to go tonight?" he asked.

Shay looked up toward the stars and then back down at

Clint. "No. But Barstow won't come after me. Not just yet anyway."

"If it's all the same to you, I'd rather keep an eye on you just to be sure. At least until this dies down a bit."

"That won't be for a while. One of Barstow's most annoying features is his long memory. I hope you weren't planning on staying in town very much longer."

Clint sighed and rounded the corner. His hotel was at the end of the next block. "I've had men after me plenty of times, but I've never let them run me out of town before. Besides, it's like I told you. I'm no good at running away from a fight once I've been thrown into it."

Shay shook her head. Although she'd only known Clint for a few hours, she knew better than to try and talk any sense into him. Once they came to the corner, she broke away from him and turned in the opposite direction. "I live down this way. If you still feel like keeping an eye on me, you can find me in the morning."

"That's too dangerous," Clint said, refusing to let go of her wrist. "You'd best come with me. I can watch you much better from my hotel room if you're in it."

Finally, the smile returned to Shay's lips, turning them up at the corners. "I was hoping you'd say that."

TWELVE

Matt Barstow stood at the bar and calmly ordered a refill of his drink. Tannen walked to one of the racks behind the bar and pulled down the right bottle. The front door slammed open, allowing Deputy Rivera to step inside, dragging behind him the fidgeting barkeep, who hadn't been quite fast enough to get away.

Barstow didn't take his eyes away from his drink. "Did you find him?"

"Got him right here," Rivera said as he shoved the barkeep into the saloon and against the bar with enough force to shake the glasses lined up on its surface.

After draining the rest of his drink, Barstow calmly set down the empty glass and turned to look at the barkeep. He regarded the other man as though he was something less than a human being. Judging by the look in his eye, Barstow might have been about to scrape something from the bottom of his boot. "How long have you worked for me?"

The barkeep swallowed hard and steadied himself with a hand against the countertop. "About a year now."

"Have I ever wronged you in any way?"

"No, sir."

"Then what did I do to deserve the treatment I received earlier this evening?"

The barkeep looked around the room with eyes that darted quickly from one man to another, surveying each of the faces

52

that were turned toward him. If he expected one of those men to be of any help, he was sadly mistaken. "I don't know . . . I guess I was just trying to help."

"Help who?" Barstow said, his voice raising to a bellowing gust that filled up every part of the saloon. "Help the man who killed Mike? Is that the man you're talking about?" Screaming now, Barstow leaned in close enough for the barkeep to feel the heat of his breath wash over his face. "Were you working with that murdering son of a bitch?"

"No! No, sir. I was just trying to help out Shay."

"I see. So, she's the one that deserves to be shot down for being a traitorous piece of garbage?"

Every part of the barkeep's body was trembling uncontrollably. Sweat poured down his face and his mouth was opening and closing like a fish that had been thrown onto the shore. "No! She was . . . I mean . . . we were . . ." Suddenly, an eerie calm descended over the barkeep's face as though he realized the hopelessness of his situation and the futility of fighting it. "Don't hurt her. Please."

"Well, then, that just leaves me one choice," Barstow said as he held his hand out toward Rivera. "I've got to hurt you."

The deputy pulled his gun and put it into Barstow's waiting hand. As soon as he did, Rivera turned his back and started walking toward the door.

Barstow didn't notice anything but the cold weight that filled his palm. When he closed his fist around the pistol, he cocked the hammer back and pressed the barrel against the barkeep's stomach. When the other man tried to move away, Tannen came up behind him and shoved the barkeep forward. As soon as he bumped against the end of the gun, he felt an explosion of pain as a hole was punched through his midsection.

The only time Barstow flinched was when he pulled the trigger. At that moment, his eyes met the barkeep's and stayed there, watching as the pain surged through the younger man's body who buckled over with his arms wrapped around his midsection. Pulling the smoking pistol back, Barstow bent at the knees so he could follow his victim to the floor without breaking eye contact.

"How's it feel?" Barstow asked.

Convulsing with pain, the barkeep slowly fell to the floor and leaned up against the side of the bar. "I'm . . . thirsty."

Barstow tilted his head as he watched the wound slowly strip away the last vestiges of life. He imagined that it was Clint Adams's face that was twisted up in silent agony like that. Imagined that he'd delivered the final bullet to end such an illustrious career.

But no matter how hard he tried, he simply couldn't get himself to truly picture what he wanted. Barstow knew himself to be a man of action, after all. Not a dreamer. The only thing that would truly appease him would be to see the real fatality played out right before his eyes.

Hacking up a wet, bloody film, the barkeep winced one more time before letting out his final breath. Only then did the hand fall away from his stomach and his head loll to the side. A strange look of peace settled over him, which disappointed Barstow to no end.

After a few minutes of quiet contemplation, Barstow stood back up and turned to look at Tannen. "What was his name?" he asked, pointing toward the corpse.

Tannen shrugged and reached for a bottle. "Hell if I know. Are we gonna go after them two or not?"

"Mister Adams isn't the type to run away under cover of darkness. Besides, he was the one to leave here with his tail between his legs, not me. If he wants to find me, he knows where to look."

"And the woman?"

Nodding slowly, Barstow licked his lips before speaking. "Now she's a different story. See if you can find her, but don't worry about Adams just yet."

"But I thought—"

Barstow wheeled around and stepped forward until his face was less than an inch away from Tannen's. "Even you can't be that stupid! You want to just chase down a man like Clint Adams when he's looking for it? Right now, he's just waiting for that very thing and you want to give it to him. Have you ever heard of Clint Adams?"

Tannen nodded.

"A man like him is just the sort of person who could put a man like me out of business," Barstow said intently. "We've got a nice little operation going here that spreads over two towns and so far, nobody seems to care. We're our own law and we govern ourselves. If we attract the wrong kind of attention, all of that comes to an end!

"And if all of that comes to an end, I'll be damned if I'm going out alone," Barstow added with a seething whisper. "Adams knows marshals and has even worked as a lawman himself. I will not allow him to ride out of my jurisdiction alive. I can't afford it."

Now it was Tannen's turn to step up. "Then why the hell did you start all of this with him to begin with? Over a damn card game? Is that worth all of this?"

The gun in Barstow's hand started moving toward Tannen's gut, but stopped short. The *click* of the hammer snapping into place echoed through the room like a clap of thunder.

But Tannen didn't seem to mind. Instead, he stepped in a little closer. "You won't shoot me," he hissed. "You need me because, unlike you, I'm not afraid to shoot at a man who isn't some scared bartender about ready to piss his pants with fear." Tannen waited until the gun was lowered before continuing. "You're right about one thing. Adams could bring an end to what we've got going. That's why we should let him have his breakfast tomorrow morning and ride the hell out."

"And if he doesn't want to leave?"

"Then we'll decide what to do. But if you want to protect your precious operation, you'd be wise to keep that mouth of yours shut and pray to god that Adams gets sick of this shithole town and rides away."

THIRTEEN

Tannen waited for Barstow to make a move against him, but after a solid minute, he knew that move would not be coming. He then stepped away and took a look around the saloon. All of the men that were left had found their way inside and were standing close at hand to witness the battle of wills taking place. Knowing that they couldn't have heard the last exchange between him and Barstow, Tannen searched their faces to see if he could tell which way each man was going to go if Barstow had made a move.

From what he could see, it was an even split between those loyal to him and those backing Barstow. If he could have been more sure about his odds, Tannen would have pulled his gun and done himself the biggest favor of his life by shutting Barstow's mouth for good. But since a bad call in this situation could have meant the end of his life, Tannen held off and started walking toward the door. Before he could get outside, he heard a familiar voice.

"I don't know what you're so upset about, anyway," Barstow said. "Killing a man like Adams could make you a right famous person. Maybe you'd get famous enough that you could live a good life somewhere outside of this shithole town without me to protect you."

Tannen's first impulse was to spin around and start beating the tar out of that fancy-dressed bastard until there wasn't anything left besides blood and pieces of bone. But then he thought about the opportunity that had presented itself in the form of Clint Adams.

All he had to do was hold his cards long enough and either Adams would kill Barstow or Tannen himself could get a good shot at Adams. Either way, Tannen came out on top.

It was a promising position to be in, but one that was going to need a little help before any results came about. For now, however, Tannen knew he needed to lay low and wait for his chance. Barstow had his uses.

Once again, Tannen started to walk out of the saloon and get himself a breath of fresh air. And once again, he was pulled back inside by the man who kept such an iron grip upon his chain.

"Before you wander off too far," Barstow said. "I want you to know something." When he saw that Tannen was paying attention, Barstow continued. "Clint Adams won't be picking up and leaving unless I want him to. Unless you forgot, I control this town and everyone inside of it."

"Oh, you'd never let me forget about that."

"Someone like Adams breezing through here and showing us up like he did today gives folks ideas. Folks like Miss Parkett and this sack of shit here," Barstow said while jabbing the barkeep's body with the toe of his boot. "If we want to keep our hold here, we need to show folks that nobody gets away with that. *Nobody*."

"So it's 'we' now, is it?"

"It can be."

Tannen leaned in the doorway, his hand resting upon his gun. "Go on."

"Make it your mission to go after Adams and I'll turn over half my interests to you and we can run things as partners. You've been my right hand long enough, we might as well make it official."

"What if I don't get a chance to kill him? I can't exactly call him out. That would be suicide."

"You don't need to kill him," Barstow said. "Just hurt him. Humiliate him in front of the folks around here enough for them to lose hope in their would-be savior. Think you can handle that?"

"For what you're offering, I'll give it one hell of a try."

*   *   *

Ellis sat in the back room, his entire body drawn up into a tight little ball and his ear pressed against the wall. He'd been at The Busted Flush waiting to buy a drink for Clint Adams in gratitude for what the man had done. He'd sent over a few beers, but Clint had been too involved in his poker game to notice.

Ellis had to remind himself that not even a full day had passed since the run-in he'd had with Tannen outside of town. Hell, it seemed as though it was a whole other lifetime ago when his life had been normal and he'd been on his way to Split Creek.

He'd been a different man back then. Back when his entire body wasn't either numb or on fire with pain. Back when he'd been just another one of the folks that Matt Barstow worked like ox in a field without giving more than a thought when one of them keeled over from the strain. Back when Tannen and his crew were just another part of everyday life.

Now, after seeing a single man stand up to Barstow, Tannen and a handful of other men as well just to keep from being cheated in a card game, Ellis was getting some different ideas in his head. At first, he'd wanted to just stay in his quiet space and wait for a good time to leave. But then he'd heard Barstow and Tannen talking and it got him thinking.

If Clint Adams knew what was being planned for him, he might just have a fighting chance of getting around it. Hell, he might even be able to go so far as to put Barstow out of business and drop Tannen like the rabid dog he was. Then maybe other folks in this town would wake up and see how they were being used instead of just sitting back and living off of whatever scraps Barstow threw to them.

Indeed, Ellis was getting some mighty big thoughts inside his head. Now all he had to do was get out of The Busted Flush without getting it blown off his shoulders.

FOURTEEN

Clint's hotel looked to be one of the better ones in town. Just the fact that it wasn't connected to a saloon made the place a step up from most of the others. It was a small room with a window overlooking a general store and blacksmith's shop. Since he'd only been into it once before to drop off his things before heading out to gamble, Clint nearly walked into the wrong room.

There were still echoes coming from James Street of raised voices and player pianos, but Clint blocked them out easily enough. Once he turned back to Shay, all he could hear was the sound of her voice.

"Guess I won't need this anymore," she said after propping her shotgun in the corner. "Or this." She slid both hands over her body and up toward her shoulders. From there, she pulled down the straps of her dress and peeled it away from her torso.

Clint stepped up close to her and ran his hands over her bare skin and then along the top of her slip. Shay's flesh was soft to the touch and the color of lightly creamed coffee. As he felt the tops of her breasts, Clint noticed something else on her skin: it was a streak of dark red left behind from the wound he'd gotten from Barstow's firing pin earlier that evening.

Looking down, Shay saw the blood and immediately

reached for Clint's hand. "Oh, you're hurt," she said soothingly as she lifted his hand to her mouth.

"It's nothing really. Just stings a little, that's all."

"Well, maybe I can make you feel better." Holding his
hand to her lips, Shay opened her mouth just enough to let
the small pink tip of her tongue reach out and run between
Clint's thumb and forefinger.

The moist, tickling sensation sent chills over Clint's skin.
And when he saw that she was looking up at him as she
tasted his flesh, the feeling became an irresistible urge to
return the favor.

Clint let her continue to gently lick his fingers as he leaned
down to taste the soft skin of her neck. Shay's hair fell in
thick strands about her shoulders, enveloping his face as he
nibbled her naked shoulders and worked his way up to her
ear. After nibbling on her earlobe, Clint brushed his lips behind it and inched his way back toward her shoulder as she
began trembling against him.

"That's better," she whispered. Moving his hand over her
body, Shay pressed his palm against her breast and arched
her back so she could kiss him passionately on the lips.

As soon as their mouths met, Clint felt her tongue slipping
over his lips and then probing deeper inside. He reached
around to hold her tight and as the kiss went on, he pulled
the slip down to her waist and ran his hands up and down
her writhing body. Shay's breasts were just the right size to
fill his hand and she moaned softly as he rubbed her nipples
with the tip of his fingers.

They worked their way over to the bed, where Shay lay
down and propped one foot up onto the mattress. The slip
fell down away from her leg, revealing a smooth expanse of
pale skin leading all the way up to the wet patch of dark
blonde hair between her thighs. She reached down between
her legs and gently caressed herself while beckoning for him
to come closer with her other hand.

Clint pulled off his shirt and quickly got out of his pants
before walking over to the side of the bed. His penis was
standing erect as he lowered himself down on top of her and
felt her legs snake around his waist. When she pulled him in

closer, the tip of his cock pressed against the soft lips between her legs.

Lying back and spreading her arms up over her head, Shay smiled luxuriously while presenting herself to him. The light from the room's single lantern played across her skin, sending ripples of shadow thrown by the material bunched up around her waist.

"You owe me, Clint Adams," she said. "I saved your life and now you've got to pay me back in kind."

Clint ran his hands along her hips and then reached beneath them to cup her firm backside. With one motion, he lifted her up off the mattress and pulled her hips in against his, burying his shaft deep inside her moist flesh. He felt her muscles constrict around him and he pushed inside just a little deeper, causing her to draw in a quick intake of breath.

"Is that enough?" Clint asked. "Or do you want more?"

Shay's smile was almost enough to light up the entire room. She closed her eyes tight and ran her fingers through her golden hair while squeezing his body between her legs. "You've got a long way to go, stud." Her voice was tinted with laughter and she punctuated what she said by running her tongue slowly over her lips.

Still holding on to her hips, Clint began working his way in and out of her, gliding within her pussy slowly at first and then building up in speed and strength. He stood at the edge of the bed and when he began pounding into her, Clint raised her lower body up a little higher so he could penetrate even deeper.

Shay began bucking against him now, her face turned to the side and her hands lightly rubbing her breasts and then down along her stomach. When she finally opened her eyes again, she reached up and grabbed Clint's wrists so she could pull him down on top of her.

Once they settled into their new position, Shay hooked first one leg over Clint's shoulder and then the next so that he could still slide inside of her as deeply as possible. As he continued thrusting, Clint could feel beads of sweat forming on his chest and back. Shay's flesh was glistening as well, her entire body writhing in time to his motions and every muscle straining with the effort.

Clint leaned over her so he could cup her breasts with both hands. As soon as his palms closed around her, Shay put her hands on top of his and began moaning softly with building intensity.

"Not yet," she whispered as she brought her legs down. "Come here."

Using her hands, she gently guided him out of her and began stroking his shaft while squirming below him. After running one finger up and down the length of his penis, she put that finger to her mouth and tasted it with the tip of her tongue.

The sight of it was nearly enough to drive Clint over the edge. And just when he thought it couldn't get any better, Shay got onto all fours and crawled forward so she could place her lips against the tip of his cock. Once again, her pink little tongue came out and she moved her head in a circle, licking her juices off of his rigid pole. After looking up at him with that gorgeous smile, she took him in his mouth and began sucking loudly.

She worked her mouth back and forth while making circles with her tongue. Clint reached down and put his hands against the back of her head, feeling it move and savoring the texture of her hair slipping between his fingers. The pleasure grew and grew until finally he exploded inside of her and had to brace himself with one hand against the mattress to keep from falling over.

When Shay pulled back, she dabbed at the corners of her mouth with her fingertips and sat with her back against the headboard. "You've just got a little more work to do before we're even," she said while spreading her legs open and gently stroking her pink lips.

Clint moved in closer and lowered his head between her thighs. "If this is what you call work, then I think I've found my perfect boss."

Shay smiled widely and rested her head against the wall as Clint's tongue began to lap up her juices. She closed her eyes again and ran her hands over his shoulders when she felt his lips upon her sensitive flesh. And when he finally buried his tongue inside of her, she dug her nails into his skin and moaned loudly.

FIFTEEN

Tannen wasn't used to thinking so hard. Even as the sun crested over the horizon, his mind still swam with all the things he and Barstow had talked about the previous day. Knowing that taking on a man like the Gunsmith could do wonders for anybody's reputation, Tannen had thought about just tracking Adams down and killing him any way he could. But then he remembered what Barstow had said and the offer he'd made. Half of Barstow's property was an awful lot. And though he knew it would never be completely his, even some of it could do a world of good.

Tannen was standing outside of the livery stable where he knew Adams was keeping his horse. There was still some chill in the air left over from the night before and the wind carried the smell of the desert. Watching over the stables from a safe distance, he mulled over those thoughts the way a cow chewed on its cud. After a while, his eyes started to droop and the effects of getting little to no sleep began to catch up to him.

He figured that since Clint's horse was still inside the livery, there was still plenty of time to catch the man. But the longer Tannen waited, the more he began to worry. No matter what plan of action he decided to take, everything hinged on him finding Adams. If Adams had somehow left town without Tannen knowing about it by taking a coach or even using a different horse, then all of Tannen's scheming could have been for nothing.

Looking over his shoulder, Tannen made sure that the two other men he'd chosen were still in position. Sure enough, one stood leaning against the front of a dry goods store and the other watched over them from atop the sheriff's office. Tannen had to smile when he saw that office. The only thing inside of it was a desk belonging to that kid, Rivera. Even the cells had been cleared out when the old lawman had been strung up the second day of Barstow's rule.

And the best part of it all was that as the townspeople walked by the gutted-out office, they didn't even bother turning their heads. It was as though the place no longer existed. There were no complaints of any kind nor even any appeals to the occasional lawman that passed through Modillo. They just went about their normal lives, too afraid to lift so much as a finger against Barstow or anyone connected to him.

Tannen would have been lying if he ever tried to say that he didn't enjoy it. Hell, he was treated like royalty wherever he went inside of Barstow's jurisdiction. That was what made taking over the boss's spot all the more appealing.

He looked back to the stables and shifted uncomfortably upon his feet. The sun was up and Adams should have been here by now, if only to check on his horse.

"Dammit," Tannen said as he spat on the ground and started walking toward the stable.

SIXTEEN

Clint walked down the street with Shay beside him, trying to ignore the grumbling coming from his stomach. His feet seemed lighter than usual after having a good night's sleep. In fact, he'd even slept in a little longer than normal and wanted to get Eclipse ready for the day's ride before stopping in for breakfast.

Although Clint was keeping an eye out for any possible trouble, Shay got more and more nervous with every step they took.

"We shouldn't be walking around in the open so much," she said as they crossed the street in front of the livery. "Barstow's not going to just let us get away this easy. He's surely sent someone after us and it's just a matter of time before—"

"Shay, look around you," Clint broke in. "Do you see anyone charging after us with guns blazing?"

She stopped and looked from side to side and then turned around to glance behind them before saying, "No."

"Then relax before you start making me jump at shadows that aren't even there. Now after I stop in here, I'm going to get some breakfast. Do you want to come with me or would you rather hide with the horses?"

"Honestly . . ."

"And just so you know, the option to hide with the horses was a joke."

"Then I guess I'll come with you."

Clint reached out and took Shay's hand. As soon as he did, she closed the distance between them and wrapped her arms around his waist. When they were standing in front of the stables, Clint stopped and looked down at her face. She looked back and gave him a halfhearted smile, but it was obvious that her fear was real for the most part.

"Is Barstow really the type of man to come at me without warning and start shooting the town apart?" he asked.

"Honestly, I don't know. I've never seen anyone go up against him like you did. But you've got to know that one of his men will be after you."

Clint put his finger beneath her chin and lifted her face up so he could plant a kiss upon her lips. The slight trembling in her muscles faded away and was replaced by the strength he'd come to expect. "I know he'll be sending someone after me, but his kind are nothing new. He's more like an animal than a man and if you run away from an animal, they'll just chase you down that much harder.

"Besides, he's not exactly the most fearsome person I've ever seen before," Clint added. His mind drifted back to all the countless others he'd met during his travels who fancied themselves to be dangerous men. More often than not, those were the ones that fell the easiest once push came to shove.

Nodding, Shay nestled into Clint's arms and gave him another quick kiss before breaking away. "I guess I've just had too much time to think since I started heading into this. Last night, I decided to help you without thinking too much about it. When we were together . . . I was running on instinct, too. And now . . ."

"Look, you don't have to get any further into this if you don't want to," Clint said. "Just say the word and I'll get on my horse and never come back here again. With me gone, Barstow should be satisfied enough for things to go back to the way they were."

"But that's just it. Things might have been quiet enough before, but it was damn sure not a good way to live."

"What do you mean?"

"Ever since Barstow moved into Modillo, he's been taking

a piece of every part of this whole town. This used to be a quiet place used as a stopover for just about every outlaw in this part of the country as they made their way south to Mexico. There were a lot of robberies and killings as one group after another rolled through.

"We finally elected a sheriff, but he was only one man and after word spread that someone was set to stand against them, the gangs started gunning for him." Shay walked to the livery and wrung her hands in front of her as a haunted look drifted across her face. "A lot of us thought Sheriff Martin would actually manage to bring some peace to this town. After all the raids that had come through here, none of us had enough money to leave and just when we started to muster up some faith in our sheriff, along comes Matt Barstow to take it all away."

Pausing with her hands held tightly in front of her, Shay looked as though the shadow that had passed over her face suddenly lifted. In its place, the darkness left behind a hard-edged strength that is only forged through surviving the worst of times. Clint wanted to try and comfort her, but he recognized that look all too well. There was nothing he could do to chase away whatever demons dwelled within her memories. The best thing he could do was hear her out.

After taking a deep breath, Shay continued. "The sheriff took out two of Barstow's men before they got to him and strung him up outside of his office. They tied his hands and feet, put the noose around his neck and let him hang at the end of a signpost."

Her eyes stared straight ahead, but saw nothing. Her voice held steady after getting just soft enough for Clint to hear it. "Didn't kill him right away, though. After letting him swing for the better part of a day, Barstow came out and started shooting at him. First his legs and then . . . other parts. Made sure the whole town saw what was happening and who was in charge, before killing him.

"After that, things actually got better. There were no more raids and life got nice and quiet. Everyone paid tribute to Barstow, but nobody seemed to mind. Kind of like a bunch of dogs that had been whipped so bad they forgot what it was like to bark on their own."

When he saw her turn to face him again, Clint noticed that the spark was back behind Shay's eyes. The memories had played themselves out and had been pushed back to where she normally kept them. "But you never settled for what Barstow offered, did you?" he asked.

Shay straightened up and steeled herself.. "No," she said with determination. "I most certainly did not."

"Then there's no reason for you to start now."

"But don't you see? That's why I wanted to tell you all of this to begin with. It's not that I want to go against Barstow. It's that nobody else in this town does." Lifting her hands up to touch Clint's cheeks, she brushed his skin and ran her fingers through his hair. "I can see that look in your eyes. Just like Sheriff Martin had. It's not your nature to let men like Barstow roll over innocent people, just like it's not in your nature to run away from a fight."

"Would you rather I left town and let Barstow's men keep you under their thumbs like you were all his property?"

"Of course not. I just want you to know what it is you're up against. If you want to take on Barstow, you won't get help from any law." Looking down the street, Shay motioned toward a few people crossing from one storefront to another. "You see them? They don't even work for Barstow, but they'll probably tell him where you're at just so the town can get back to normal."

Clint stared into her eyes and shook his head. "And what makes you think I'm about to go through all this trouble for a town I've only spent one night in?"

Shay looked away just then, ashamed. "Because you stood against him once and won. Because you're a fighter."

SEVENTEEN

Clint didn't mind hearing those words coming from Shay's mouth. And he most certainly didn't mind the way she looked at him when she'd said them. But as much as he enjoyed the compliment, he couldn't help but feel embarrassed by it. "You have some mighty romantic notions about me," he said. "Especially when I might not have made it out of that saloon without your help."

"Don't take me for a fool, Clint. I saw the way you moved in there. If you hadn't done so much talking, you could've shot down every last one of those men."

"Maybe."

"You wouldn't have even had to kill them all. Just beating him again might be enough to get people to see that Barstow isn't invincible. That his men aren't tough enough to keep an entire town beneath their heels."

Clint noticed that Shay had begun to breathe faster and fidget on her feet as her voice became more and more excited with every passing word. He put his hands upon her shoulders and made sure she was looking directly into his eyes before he spoke. "Are you asking me for my help?"

For a second, she seemed genuinely stumped by the question. Waiting for a bit, Shay seemed almost put back by the simplicity of it. Then she took a breath and said, "Well . . . yes."

"If I do this, you've got to know that I'm not a gun for

hire. I'll do things my way and if you want to help me, you've got to do exactly what I say. Do you understand?"

She nodded as her eyes began brightening.

Clint had gotten it in his head to work against Barstow the moment he realized that the man was connected to the gang that had been harassing Ellis outside of town. Just by watching Barstow and Tannen work, it was plain to see that they had their hooks deep into Modillo and were not about to let go.

Clint had already found out the hard way that Deputy Rivera wasn't about to stand against Barstow. The fact that there wasn't a sheriff just made it that much more important in Clint's mind that he take a stand against the gang.

The fact that there wouldn't be much of anyone else in town that could help him didn't bother Clint too much either. He'd seen the kind of threat Barstow posed and frankly, Clint wasn't too impressed. Besides, he wasn't much of one to ask for a lot of help anyway.

"So where do we start?" Shay asked, her voice and features filled with anxious energy.

Clint ushered her inside the stable and made sure there was nobody coming in behind them. "I was going to start with some breakfast, but it sounds like we'd be better off just getting a move on and eating along the way."

"We're still leaving?" she asked, not even trying to mask her disappointment.

"The more I think about it, the more I see that the best thing for us to do is ride out of here as fast as we can. In fact, if there's a way out of town that uses the busiest streets or even goes past The Busted Flush, that's all the better."

"But why should we take off like a couple of dogs with our tails between our legs?"

Clint spun around and pointed a finger at her. "Because that's exactly what we want Barstow to see. Right now, he's expecting me to make my move and call him out. He's ready for it and so are all of his men. From what he's probably heard about me, Barstow's more than likely ready to make a stand behind all of the guns he can call to his side."

As Shay listened, the smile on her face grew wider. Nodding as Clint spoke, she walked up close to him and slid her arms around his waist. "But if he thinks we're running scared, he'll let his guard down."

"And that," Clint said, "is when I can get close to him."

Shay looked around the stables and her eyes locked upon a small figure that was running toward them as though its tail was on fire. When Clint looked over there, he immediately recognized the young boy who'd taken Eclipse's reins the other day.

"Are you here to check on your horse, mister?" the kid asked.

"Actually, I need to take him out," Clint said as he headed toward the correct stall. "I'm leaving town."

The boy's face nearly dropped to the floor where it would get lost amid all the straw. "But . . . we had a deal."

"Don't worry. You can keep the money." Looking over Eclipse, Clint saw that the Darley Arabian had already been brushed and groomed. Judging by the look in the stallion's eyes, he'd probably also been well fed and exercised. "It looks like you've earned every penny."

The kid reached out to pat Eclipse on the muzzle. "He's the best horse I ever seen. All we usually get are old nags and worn-out pack mules." Suddenly, the boy's entire body twitched and his head snapped up to look at Clint. "I nearly forgot to tell you!"

"Tell me what?"

"There was some fella who came around here askin' about you."

Shay stepped up and put her hand on the boy's shoulder. "Did you recognize him?"

"Sure did. He's one of them that rides with Tannen. I seen him talking to Mister Barstow on occasion as well. He tried to do something to this horse, but I wouldn't let him."

Clint got busy laying a blanket over Eclipse's back and then strapping on the saddle. "What did he want to know about me?"

"He asked me if I knew where you was staying or when you'd be leaving."

"What did you tell him?"

"Not much. He gave me some money, but it wasn't half as much as what you already paid me. Besides, those men can rot in hell for all I care."

"Watch your mouth," Shay said in a scolding, motherly tone.

Reflexively, the kid lowered his head and rolled his eyes as though he'd been swatted on the nose. "Sorry, ma'am. But my pa says those men should be strung up after what they did to Sheriff Martin."

Clint finished up with what he was doing. Eclipse fussed a little, but mainly because he seemed anxious to get outside. "Take it easy, boy," Clint said soothingly. "You'll get your chance soon enough." To the kid, he said, "Think you can run to my hotel and fetch my saddlebags?"

The kid nodded enthusiastically. "Yes, sir."

Tossing a quarter down to him, Clint added, "Be back here quick enough and there'll be another one of those waiting for you."

Before the words had fully escaped Clint's mouth, the boy was running for the door and kicking up a cloud of dust behind his feet. Clint laughed to himself and walked over to the stable's front door.

"You look like you're enjoying this," Shay said as she stroked Eclipse's neck.

"Would you feel better if I acted how I really felt?"

"And how's that?"

"Hungry. I'm about ready to taste some of what's in that feedbag if I don't get some food in my belly."

Shay gave him a playful slap on the shoulder. "I'm being serious here, Clint. You look about as happy now as you did when you were playing poker the other night. Well, before they started shooting at you, anyway."

Turning his attention completely onto her, Clint took Shay in his arms and gave her a kiss that nearly dropped them down to the straw and tore the clothes right off of their backs. When he was finally able to pull himself away, Shay reached her hands around him and kept him rooted to the spot. They stayed there for another few minutes, enjoying the taste of each other on their lips and the feel of the other's body against their own. When both of them took a step back, it was due more to a need to catch their breath than anything else.

"What was that for?" Shay asked.

"For the same reason that I want to help you and the people of this town. Because I felt like it."

"You're gonna put your life on the line for a bunch of strangers because you felt like it? Not to sound ungrateful, but . . ."

Clint smiled and shrugged his shoulders. "That's about all it ever boils down to. You want to follow the rules or break them? Improve your life or stay the same? Obey duty or go your own way? It all boils down to which one you feel like doing. I've learned that people say a lot of things, but they'll do whatever the hell they feel like doing and then come up with a reason later."

"When did you come up with this?"

"I've been riding a lot lately. Gives me plenty of time to think." Clint could hear footsteps pounding on the boardwalk as they got closer to the stables. Before checking outside, however, he kept focused on Shay. Mainly, he looked for any sign of doubt within the watery blue depths of her eyes.

He had no trouble believing what she'd said about the majority of the town being more or less on Barstow's side. He needed to make sure that she wasn't going to head that way as well. "What I really need to know," Clint said, "is what you feel like doing. You've put yourself on the line for me once, but if you're seen riding out of town with me, there won't be any going back."

"There's already no going back for me. Once I lifted a finger against Barstow, I sealed my fate. All I've got in this town is my saloon and Barstow's set to take that away and use it up just like he did with every other business in town." Shay took a deep breath and steeled herself against the fear tickling the edge of her thoughts. "So are we gonna get going or keep talking all day?"

EIGHTEEN

Tannen sat outside of the livery just as he had for the last several hours. When he'd finally seen Adams and the woman from The Busted Flush go inside, he thought there was certainly going to be an end to his waiting. But once the pair had disappeared inside the stable, the minutes seemed to drag by that much slower.

He was half tempted to kick down the door to the livery just to break the boredom when something caught his eye. At that moment, the stable boy rushed toward the livery from down the street, his arms full with what looked like one or two bags. A few minutes later, the doors were pulled open and Adams came riding out on that stallion of his as though he'd set the barn on fire.

Watching as the Darley Arabian thundered past, Tannen was certain that Adams looked straight at him as he was passing by. It was at that moment that Tannen saw the blonde woman sitting on the back of the saddle with her arms wrapped tightly around Adams's torso.

Tannen didn't have much use for subtlety anymore and he ran down the street, cutting through an alley so that he could possibly get to The Busted Flush before Adams flew by the place.

He was out of breath and wheezing noisily by the time he reached the saloon. The pounding of the stallion's hooves grew louder as Clint approached the nearby corner.

"Mister Barstow," Tannen shouted with all the energy he could muster. "You . . . you got to come out here quick."

Barstow was standing at the end of the bar nursing a cup of coffee and regarding Tannen with mild disinterest. "What the hell are you talking about?"

"It's Adams. He—"

That was all that needed to be said before Barstow was heading toward the front door. By the time he stepped outside, Barstow saw Adams ride past as fast as the horse could carry him without endangering the lives of folks trying to cross the street. Barstow half expected the other man to turn his horse around and head back, but instead Clint kept right on going until he was headed straight for the edge of town.

"Well, I'll be damned," Barstow said. "What brought that on?" Turning to look at Tannen he asked, "Did he say anything about where he was going?"

Tannen had gotten some of his wind back, but not enough to stand up straight without putting his hands on his hips for support. "Nope. I was just keeping track of him like you said and then he came busting out of there. Should I go after him?"

Barstow nodded toward the horse tied up in front of the building. "Saddle up and pick up his trail. It shouldn't be too hard since there ain't much else in that direction by way of cover. I'll send a few men after you."

What little energy Tannen had saved up was gone by the time he sprinted over to his brown mare and climbed onto the saddle. He whipped the reins across the animal's back and held on as the mare broke into a run and tore off in Clint's wake.

Barstow watched the other man go, admiring the way Tannen snapped to as though he'd received a command from the almighty himself. He'd been expecting a lot of things from Adams, but running for the hills wasn't one of them. On one hand, he had to be just a little proud for being able to run the Gunsmith out of his town. On the other, Barstow knew better than to think he'd won so easily.

Nothing in this life was to be had without its share of complications. And this was far too simple to be over.

Barstow stood outside, enjoying the feeling of the morning sun on his face and the taste of coffee on his tongue. Even if it wasn't the end of his dealings with Clint Adams, it still felt mighty good to see someone like him running in the other direction. Barstow enjoyed the taste of power it gave him, no matter how fleeting it was, and then turned to walk back inside.

"Rivera," he called to the Mexican sitting over his breakfast at one of the back tables. "Round up some men and head north out of town. You should run into Tannen somewhere not too far and he might not be alone."

"Adams?" the deputy asked.

"He was heading out of town in a rush. Just make sure that wherever he is, he's not trying anything."

"What should I do when I find him?"

"Just watch for now. If he gets too far away, let him go. If he makes camp or doubles back, come tell me about it."

Once again, Barstow stood aside and watched as someone else sprung into action and danced to the tune he'd played. Modillo's deputy sheriff, the closest thing that town had to any kind of law, set aside his food and rushed out of the saloon just like a dog who'd been told to fetch a stick.

Part of Barstow wondered if Adams hadn't just gotten out of town to avoid being outgunned ten to one. Indeed, Barstow had one hell of a greeting in mind if the legendary Gunsmith decided to show his face in the wrong place again. Surely, a man like Clint Adams had bigger things to worry about than a town like this one, but then again . . . another part of Barstow's mind wished Adams would try his luck.

That part whispered congratulations into his ear about standing toe to toe with a legend and forcing that man to blink. A crooked smile worked its way onto Barstow's face like a reptile wriggling its way out from beneath a desert rock. In the end, it really didn't seem to matter what the explanation was for Adams leaving. As long as he stayed gone, Barstow didn't much care for the man's reason.

As Rivera and the rest of Tannen's men rode away from the saloon and headed for the edge of town, Barstow leaned against the bar and savored the rest of his drink. It tasted good . . . like victory.

Once Tannen was away from Modillo and on the open trail, spotting Adams was not very hard at all. The other man's horse was still going fast enough to kick up a cloud of dust that made his stand out just as plainly as the sun in the sky. Allowing his pace to ease off a bit, Tannen kept his eye on that dust cloud and soon heard the sound of horses coming up behind him.

He turned in the saddle and spotted five familiar riders headed his way. Once they were close enough, he raised a hand and waited for Rivera to come up alongside of him.

"That him up ahead?" the deputy asked.

"Yeah. Looks like he's probably headed for Split Creek. There ain't much else that direction besides the desert."

Rivera nodded. "I'd say he's headed for another town since this one's full of nothing but bad intentions as far as he's concerned."

"He had Shay with him."

The deputy cocked his head and squinted into the distance as though he'd be able to spot the blonde amid the dusty haze. "Really? Are you sure?"

"Saw her with my own eyes."

"You think she might be trying to help him?"

Tannen shrugged. "She can't do anything that he wouldn't be able to do. She's probably just catching a ride into Split Creek to avoid the beating that would be coming for what she did inside that saloon. I say we follow them halfway to Split Creek and if they don't change direction, we'll head on back."

All of Tannen's men seemed more than happy about that idea. Even Rivera nodded enthusiastically upon hearing the suggestion. As a second thought, however, the deputy stared at the shrinking dust cloud.

"What if he doubles back?" he asked.

"He won't."

"Are you sure about that?"

Just then, Tannen turned in his saddle until he was facing

the deputy head-on. He leaned forward like a hungry animal as a snarl pulled at the edges of his lips. All around him, his men shifted on their horses with their hands inching toward their guns, recognizing the familiar look on their leader's face.

"I'll tell you what I am sure of," Tannen growled. "I'll sure as hell beat the living shit out of you if you keep questioning me at every turn. You may have been the law here, but you don't have any say over what I do. Understand that?"

Rivera locked his eyes onto Tannen's without giving an inch as the other man lit into him.

"Adams is runnin' scared," Tannen continued. "I can smell it. And if you think for one minute that I'm letting that one get too far away from me, than you've been spending way too much time with your feet propped up on that desk of yours back in town. We're going after Adams and I'll be the one to skin the hide off his cowardly bones."

"Barstow told me that—"

"Barstow don't want nothin' besides that town and he can kiss my ass if he tries to keep me from an opportunity like this one. It ain't too often that a man like the Gunsmith turns tail and runs. Maybe he is scared or maybe he just don't want to bother himself with the likes of us, but whichever it is, I plan on making him sorry he ever turned his back on me." When Tannen saw that the deputy wasn't about to say anything else, he turned his attention back to the trail ahead and touched the spurs to his horse's side.

Rivera let Tannen and his cowboys ride on ahead. He thought about following the men and even standing by Tannen's side when he took on Clint Adams. But there was something about following a dirty fool like that into a fight that just didn't sit right with the young deputy. Barstow had told him to follow until he knew where Adams was going and the answer to that question was obvious.

As far as what would happen once Adams and Tannen met up in Split Creek, Rivera knew damn well that the Gunsmith wouldn't be taken without a fight. That part of Rivera's mind now caused him to rein in his horse and turn it back toward Modillo.

"Fuck him," he grumbled under his breath. "He can get himself killed for all I care, but I sure as hell won't go with him."

The next few hours passed without more than three words exchanged between all of the men. Tannen hardly even noticed that Rivera wasn't among them as he followed Clint's trail east. It was obvious that he was going to Split Creek and Tannen was more than happy to follow him there.

NINETEEN

Even without seeing the horses behind him, Clint could feel them following in Eclipse's wake as though their eyes were burning holes into the back of his neck. He didn't draw his weapons right away, but he kept his hand poised over the rifle at his side, just waiting for any reason at all to pull the gun and get to work.

During the bulk of the ride, Clint's brain was screaming at him to go for the rifle and be ready for the attack that should be coming at any minute. Clint managed to somehow fight back that initial reaction to draw the rifle and at least make sure that his rear was covered simply because he knew they would never be able to catch him. Even with two riders on his back, Eclipse was more than a match for what those cowboys had. So rather than worry about them, he kept going at full speed to the town of Split Creek, New Mexico.

Even as he got within sight of the town, Clint waited for an attack from Tannen or his men. The longer it took for that attack to get there, the more on edge he felt.

Finally, they got to a point where Tannen was either going to attack or risk losing his advantage before Clint made it into town limits. And when that point had come and gone, it was obvious that there was no attack coming.

Turning in the saddle, Clint looked over his shoulder and past the woman who sat with her face buried against his shirt. Coming up from behind him, floating amid a dusty mist that resembled a dirty ghost, was somewhere around half a dozen or more men that had been with him since he'd left Modillo.

Whatever their reasons for not attacking, it didn't much matter to Clint. He'd been ready for a fight during the entire ride, but that wasn't how they were going to play it. More than likely they were trying to figure out his own reasons for leaving Modillo in such a rush. Well, they would have to figure out that one on their own. Smiling, Clint somewhat enjoyed the notion of driving his pursuers a little crazy. After all, that was as good a place as any to start in on his own assault.

"Are they still back there?" Shay asked in a voice that reflected the tension she'd felt during the entire ride into Split Creek.

"Yeah, they're back there," Clint replied. "But it looks like they won't be starting anything just yet. They probably want to make sure we're planning on staying here rather than doubling back and driving back down Barstow's throat."

"And is that what we're going to do?"

"As far as they know . . . yes."

They were just now pulling to a stop near some buildings marking the border of Split Creek and Shay was all but jumping down off of Eclipse's back.

"Good," she said. "Then I can get off of this thing before it throws me off. I swear my brains are about to slide out of my ear after being rattled in that saddle for so long."

Clint reined Eclipse to a full stop and offered his hand to help her climb down to the ground. "Do you know your way around this place?"

"Well enough to find us a place to stay."

"What about the livery?"

She gave him directions to the closest stable as well as a good place to stop for something to eat. They hadn't slowed down for more than a minute or two during the entire ride, not to mention the fact that they'd completely abandoned the prospect of stopping for something to eat as Clint had promised.

"Sorry about that," Clint said when she brought up their missed breakfast with a cranky scowl on her face. "But I didn't think you'd want to eat with Tannen and his men breathing down our backs like that."

"You're sure that was Tannen following us?"

"No matter how I sped up or slowed down during our ride here, those men stayed the same distance behind us the entire time. Seeing as how we would have left behind any regular travelers in the dust, I'd say that those men were definitely following us. I don't see Barstow as the type of man who does his own work as long as there's somebody else to do it for him, so that only leaves Tannen as the one who would get the duty of dogging us all the way from Modillo."

Shay turned around in a quick circle, nervously glancing about as though she fully expected the gunman to be right behind her. "Are they still here?" she asked.

"No, they broke off sometime before we pulled into town."

"How could you tell?"

"Your ears get used to the sound of your own horse after a while. I couldn't hear much, but with that many men following us on an open trail, you can pick up enough of a sound to know they're there." Clint could tell the blonde was admiring him with those beautiful blue eyes.

"You're an impressive man, Clint Adams."

"You tend to pick up a few tricks when you ride the trail long enough. Especially when you look over your shoulder as much as I do."

Shay's face darkened a bit when she thought about that, but she quickly shook it off and looked around at the surrounding street. The afternoon sun was high in the sky and it beat down unmercifully upon her exposed neck and shoulders. It was a dry heat that baked rather than stewed, but it was still hot just the same.

Split Creek looked to be much quieter than Modillo. At least, that's what Clint could tell from what little of the town he could see. The place just had a more sedate feel to it when compared to the other town's gambling atmosphere. Of course all of that might change as soon as night fell, but it made Clint feel better to think that he might actually get some peace and quiet for a change.

Once she got her bearings, Shay pointed to a nearby corner. "That's Main Street," she said. "Head down that way and meet me at the Sampson Inn. We should be safe there more than any other place in town."

"How much influence does Barstow have in Split Creek?"

"Not as much as in Modillo, but that's just because he doesn't live here."

"Is there a real sheriff in town?"

Shay thought about that for a minute and then nodded. "Sheriff Furlan was the last one I heard about. At least, I think he should still be somewhere around here."

Clint had pretty much figured that a town so close to Modillo wouldn't be completely out of Barstow's grasp. All he needed was to give the right impression and buy himself some time. Hopefully, the residents of Split Creek wouldn't be as prepared to hand him over as long as he kept his head down and stayed out of trouble.

"I only need another day or two," he said. "Do you think we'll be all right here for that long?"

Once again, she nodded. Only this time she didn't seem quite so sure. "I guess. What do you need to do here?"

Reflexively, Clint's hand went to the damaged gun at his side. "First I need some tools. There's a repair job that I can't put off any longer."

"And then what? We go back to Modillo?"

"You can stay here if you want. Actually, that might be a better idea if you stayed put until things there get settled once and for all."

"But those people are under Barstow's thumb," Shay said with a definite edge to her voice. "They wouldn't help you before. Hell, half those people at The Busted Flush just drew down on you because Barstow looked at them the wrong way. They deserve to stay there and lick his boots just like they've always done."

"They're just scared, Shay. And they're not gunfighters. If they were, they would have seen that they had me dead to rights back there and could've killed me on the spot. But they didn't fire. Not to kill anyway. And that saved my life just as well as you did."

It was strange to see Shay's expression change from anger

to amusement in the blink of an eye. Shaking her head, she gave a little laugh and said, "You wouldn't have let them kill you. I saw enough of the way you moved to know that for a fact."

"That could be. But they didn't know that. The point is that they didn't try to kill me. I've had enough people try that I can recognize that look in the eye. Only Barstow, Tannen and a few of the men had it. The rest were just keeping up appearances."

Grudgingly, Shay nodded. "Guess I'm just sick of living with a bunch of sheep."

"Well, there's one way to take care of that," Clint said as he pulled out his Colt and surveyed the damage with a professional eye. "You get rid of the shepherd."

TWENTY

Clint was able to find most of the tools he needed after making his way to several of Split Creek's craftsmen. Eventually, he found a local store owner who had a large selection of Colts, Winchesters and the occasional Henry. The storekeeper was no smith, but he did have most of the tools Clint needed. A few dollars placed upon the older man's counter was enough to convince him to let Clint borrow the tools for the next few days.

When he got back to the Sampson Inn, it was nearly two o'clock and Shay was nowhere to be found. Clint didn't really expect her to stay alone in her room all day, so he checked in with the man at the front desk who handed over the key Shay had left for him. Once he was upstairs, Clint went to his room and set his things down next to the bed.

There was a small chest of drawers on the other side of the bed and a round table set between two wooden stools. Clint cleared off the small table near the window and spread a cloth over its surface to create a space for him to get to work. Once all the tools were laid out so he could get to any one of them, he took out his modified Colt and began disassembling it piece by piece.

The first thing he did once the gun was apart was to use another cloth and some oil to clean up each component and decide which were fine and which needed to be repaired in order for the gun to fire accurately. From what he could see, when he'd been shot at those days ago, the bullet grazed off the side of the gun, denting the cylinder and damaging the firing mechanism. The end result was that the chambers weren't revolving between shots and the firing pin wasn't hitting the cartridge straight on. So far, the gun hadn't been able to fire at all. If it did manage to get a shot off, chances were good that the round would jam in the chamber or get wedged in the barrel. After that, the next thing to happen would be for the whole thing to blow up, taking most of his hand right along with it.

It felt good to let his mind focus in on the tasks required to fix the Colt. Clint allowed his hands to go about their duties as though they had minds of their own. The pieces of the gun flowed between his fingertips like little parts to a puzzle and when one didn't fit properly, he grabbed a nearby tool and set about the job of repairing the damage.

For the most part, the cylinder and hammer mechanism had taken the brunt of the bullet's impact. Clint thought back to the last time he'd fired the pistol as he continued fitting it back together.

It had happened in Colorado. There was an incident there where a boxer had gotten himself into more trouble than he could handle and was trying to get away from it so he could start a new life with his sister and nephew. If Clint hadn't stopped in to watch the fights, he never would have gotten involved with the boxer. As it was, he managed to get into the other man's trouble up to his ears and nearly got himself shot in the process.

The only thing that had saved him was the Colt. When Clint had seen that someone was about to take a shot at the boxer, he'd tried to get the other man clear and took a bullet in the hip . . . right where the Colt had been hanging. That gun had saved his life more than once, but usually in a different style.

As Clint worked on the damaged parts, he thought about all the time he'd spent piecing the weapon together and even creating the special modifications that brought the pistol over from single-action to double-action. That gun fit as though it had been created for his hand. It was a part of him just as

vital as the heart that beat in his chest or the breath in his
lungs. Using the other weapons in Modillo seemed more than
just awkward. It had seemed wrong.

Every time he'd rode into a town since Colorado, Clint
had been looking to get his hands on the proper tools to fix
his Colt. But most of those towns were mining camps or
temporary settlements that were lucky to get the supplies they
needed to live. If something happened to their guns, they got
new ones or fixed them themselves.

Clint thought back to the days he used to ply his trade
from the back of a wagon. It had felt good to do an honest
day's work in a normal job. Even though it had been some
time since he'd worked as a real gunsmith, Clint worked with
the Colt's pieces as if he was still in the back of that wagon
with oil on his fingers and tools scattered in front of him.

When he found pieces that just needed to be cleaned or
repaired, Clint did just that and fit them back together. The
cylinder and hammer, on the other hand, were too far gone
to be saved. The metal was scorched and bent so severely
that it would take more than he had to pound them back
again. Such efforts would probably only break the pieces
anyway.

He put aside the partially completed Colt and set the other
two guns he'd acquired onto the cloth. After disassembling
those, he sifted through the pieces and began scrutinizing
them carefully.

One of the guns was an old chunk of metal that was better
off at the bottom of a scrap heap. The only thing that had
made it perform well at all was that it hadn't been fired too
much recently. In fact, Clint was glad he hadn't tried to get
off more than a few shots with the thing.

The second gun was a different story. That one was a bit
newer and looked as though it was much better cared for.
Thinking back to the men he'd seen at the poker table, Clint
figured that gun must have belonged to one of Tannen's men.
The pieces came apart easily in Clint's expert hands. Although it wasn't the same model, the gun was a Colt and
could be used for spare parts to replace the ones Clint
needed.

It wasn't a simple matter of trading one piece for another, but making the switch only required a bit of tool work. For Clint, it was barely work at all. The time flew by as he made the necessary adjustments and finally fit the pieces onto his own pistol. He slid a few bullets into the chamber and gave the cylinder a spin, putting it close to his ear so he could hear every well-oiled click.

The motion wasn't as smooth as he would have liked, but it would serve in a pinch. All he needed to make it perfect was some more time with the tools. In fact, Clint was glad that the gun still needed some extra work.

Just as he was about to dismantle the Colt a second time, the sound of footsteps drifted in from the hall outside and stopped in front of his door. His eyes narrowed as he concentrated on whether or not the sounds could have belonged to Shay.

Clint was about to call her name when the person outside took another step closer toward the door. Besides the footsteps being a little too heavy for a woman, they also seemed unsure as to which door was the right one. Shay would know where her own room was located and would have definitely been inside by now.

Looking down at the table, Clint began locating the pieces he needed to assemble at least one functioning weapon. His hands flashed between the components and fit them together just as the door handle started wiggling back and forth. When the latch pulled back and the door started to swing inward, Clint's hands were full.

His right fist was clenched around a handle and his left was filled with another pistol's barrel. When those heavy footsteps began charging into the room, the first thing Clint could see was the barrel of the stranger's gun. Clint only hoped he could be holding a functioning pistol by the time the man took his next step.

TWENTY-ONE

Clint's hands flashed together as he raced to get the pistol put together before the stranger took a full step inside his room. He heard the *snap* of one half fitting inside the other just as the stranger was moving beyond the door. Clint realized the cylinder only contained two shots as he closed the weapon and pulled back the hammer.

He'd never seen the other man before, Clint realized as soon as he got a look at the person's face. The next thing he saw was the stranger's eyes tracking toward him as both of them started taking quick aim and raising their guns.

A shot roared within the confines of the hotel room and a puff of smoke drifted toward the ceiling. The stranger's entire body twitched at the sound, but not fast enough to avoid getting hit by the piece of lead that headed his direction. Pain lanced from the fresh hole in his chest and the slug spun him around in a tight quarter-circle.

Clint was about to command the other man to set his gun onto the floor, but noticed the stranger was fighting through the pain and already less than a second away from taking his shot. Clint pulled back the hammer again and squeezed the trigger. This time, all he got in response from the metal in his hand was the *click* of a pin falling into an empty chamber.

With that sound still echoing through his ears, Clint pitched himself to the side just as fire belched from the stranger's weapon. The bullet tore through the air like an angry wasp, missing Clint by less than a foot and burying itself deep into the opposite wall.

This time, Clint remembered the New Line that was stuck in his belt. The gun didn't weigh much, and was one he only used in emergencies, but this qualified. He drew the gun and fired instinctively. The sound of lead slapping against flesh was unmistakable, as was the whine of a bullet whipping through the air near Clint's head, which followed soon after. As soon as he threw himself to the side, Clint's first reaction was to check himself over for any fresh bullet holes. He didn't feel any pain, but that didn't necessarily mean he wasn't hit. After rolling to one side, he patted himself down with one hand and quickly realized that it hadn't been him who'd just been shot.

Clint looked back up and got ready to fire when he noticed the stranger had already dropped to one knee. Besides the hole in his chest that Clint had given him, the other man also had a messy wound just below his neck that leaked a steady stream of blood down the front of his shirt. Rather than take aim from his new position, the other man winced, let out the breath he'd been holding and fell facefirst to the floor. He landed heavily with his eyes wide open, staring up disbelievingly at Clint.

Knowing better than to watch the stranger, Clint turned his attention toward the doorway and the source of the last shot. He got first to his knees and then up into a low crouch as another set of footsteps made its way inside.

"Come on in here where I can see you," Clint ordered as he sighted down his barrel.

Just as he was about to make the command a second time, he saw something land on the floor just inside the doorway. It was a pistol. Walking in behind it with his hands held up high was a familiar figure with long, gray hair and tough, leathery skin.

"Ellis?" Clint said as he nearly put a bullet into the old man's hide. "What the hell are you doing here?"

TWENTY-TWO

At first, the old man had trouble saying much of anything. But when Clint lowered his gun and motioned for him to come inside, Ellis's voice started returning to him. "I tried to catch up with you back in Modillo, but Tannen and his men were waiting to catch sight of you and I didn't exactly feel like giving them another target in the meantime. When I went to find you this morning, you and Miss Parkett had already left."

Clint held his gun at hip level, walked past Ellis and took a quick look in the hallway. As far as he could tell, there was nobody else waiting to make another surprise entrance. Once he was back inside his room and behind a locked door, Clint looked down at the stranger, who was sprawled out on his floor.

The first thing he noticed was the hole between the other man's shoulder blades. Using the toe of his boot, Clint rolled the stranger onto his side so he could get a better look at his face. Nothing about the other man struck a chord in Clint's mind. "Do you know who this man is?" he asked.

Ellis did his best not to look at the body and instead walked over to the window and stuck his head outside. After breathing in a few times to clear his head, he looked over his shoulder at Clint. "He's one of Barstow's."

"They must have followed me all the way here after all. I thought I'd lost them somewhere between Modillo and here."

Looking more than a little pale around the edges, Ellis kept his head up and his eyes away from the body on the floor. "That one lives here in Split Creek. He's one of the killers that Barstow uses to represent his interests outside of Modillo. As far as I know, I was the only one who followed you all the way here."

Clint checked the man over and pulled the gun from the stranger's hand.

"Is . . . is he . . ." Ellis stammered.

"He's dead, all right. You're one hell of a shot."

"I . . . didn't mean to hurt no one. I just wanted to catch up to you and let you know that Barstow was gonna be coming after you with all he's got. Since I couldn't catch up to you in Modillo, I waited for you to go to get your horse, but Tannen was waiting for you outside of there as well. After you took off, it looked like you and Miss Parkett were headed this way and since I been trying to get here for a few days, I just headed this way myself."

"Then you were behind that stagecoach I saw on the trail behind us?" Clint asked, testing to see if Ellis would answer correctly.

The old man looked confused for a second and shook his head. "No . . . I thought you would'a known that . . . that Tannen and his men were behind you most of the way here."

It was hard to believe that someone as rattled as Ellis could pull himself together well enough to lie with any conviction, but Clint felt it was better to test the waters just to be safe. Now that he was sure, he said, "Most of the way?"

"Yeah. They broke off when they were almost here and headed back for Modillo. Probably to check in with Barstow. All he has to do is send one word by telegraph and his men will go after anyone for him in any of the towns he controls."

Satisfied that Ellis was telling the truth, Clint relaxed slightly and dropped the gun into his holster. "Better take a seat, Ellis. You're shaking like a leaf in a stiff wind."

Just then, more footsteps began pounding through the hallway outside, soon to be followed by rapping on Clint's door.

"What's going on in there?" came the muffled voice of

the man who worked behind the counter in the lobby. "Were those gunshots?"

Clint went over and opened the door. "We had some trouble. You'd better get the sheriff."

The hotel's owner looked past Clint, his eyes growing wide when he spotted the body on the floor. "I'll be right back," he said before turning and running back down the stairs.

Clint turned to Ellis and asked, "Is the law in this town any better than what's in Modillo?"

"A little," Ellis replied. "But he still answers to Barstow eventually."

"Then I figure we've got a few minutes to clear out of here and move on."

"What's that?"

Clint was already scooping up his gear and stowing it inside his saddlebags along with the gun parts and tools he'd borrowed. In just under a minute, the only thing that marked he'd been there was the body on the floor. "Barstow's had plenty of time to run his games and stack his decks against the folks around here. I've beaten him once already despite the odds and I'm about to do it again."

"You think you can deal me in this time?" Ellis asked as the color began seeping back into his face.

Clint studied the old man carefully. "Are you sure you want in on this? You know better than I do that this could get rough real quickly." Pointing down to the body on the floor, he added, "Even rougher than it's already gotten."

"You don't have to tell me that. I've been living under Barstow and his men for a while now. That's why I want to help you."

"We'll discuss this in a little bit," Clint said as he hefted his saddlebags over his shoulder and walked for the door. "But first, do you know if there's another way out of this place?"

Ellis pointed down toward the back of the hallway. "There's a set of stairs that lead into the alley. If you take those, the only folks that'll spot you would be the ones in the kitchen."

"You make a lot of escapes from this place, Ellis?"

"Just from the wife." When he noticed the amused look he was getting from Clint, the old man added, "There's a redhead that does her business in this hotel. Been seein' her for a few months now." Besides the color coming back into his face, there was now some extra red in his cheeks as well. "I'm not always spending my time chasin' after gunfighters, you know."

Clint let out a little laugh and stepped into the hall. "Lead the way, loverboy. And try not to get diverted when you reach the end of the hall."

The two rushed past the other rooms and quickly spotted the narrow staircase stuck next to the last door like an afterthought. The steps were so small that Clint had to step sideways as he climbed down them. More than once, his feet nearly slipped out from under him but he managed to make it to the bottom without breaking his neck. Ellis, on the other hand, seemed to fly down the stairs with practiced ease.

"Why do I get the feeling that you'd have been running down these stairs later tonight even if I hadn't shown up?" Clint asked.

Ellis started to look offended, but couldn't quite pull it off. "Just be thankful we didn't have to take my other way out of there," he said while nodding toward a window on the second floor.

TWENTY-THREE

It had been a long time since Shay had been all the way to Split Creek. Although she hadn't thought about it on the way over, once she got to town and started wandering the streets after checking into the hotel, she realized just how many people she'd left behind the last time she'd been forced to leave for Modillo.

There were the people who owned the restaurant on Sacramento Avenue, the shopkeepers she'd known since her teen years down on Third, and of course the owners of the Flat Jack Saloon who'd taught her everything she knew about running a business. If it wasn't for all those people, she would have walked back to the Sampson Inn much earlier.

That way, she just might have caught a glimpse of the man that walked into the hotel with the murderous look in his eyes. She might have heard the gunshots coming from the second floor minutes later. And she just might have caught up with Clint as he'd slipped out the back way.

As it was, she was just in time to see Sheriff Furlan run into the front door without so much as a how-do-you-do. Shay stepped aside to let the lawman pass and then put her hand on the knob to step inside herself.

"Shay," came a whispered voice from the alley to her right.

At first, she merely paused and stared at the wood grain

of the front door, waiting to see if she'd imagined the sound or if someone really had just said her name.

"Dammit, Shay. Turn around."

There was no mistaking it that time. She'd heard the wind make strange noises before, but it never once swore at her.

Still standing with the door half open, Shay turned toward the alley and nearly called out Clint's name when she saw him peeking from between the buildings. She held her tongue, however, when she saw the urgent look on his face and the way he waved for her to hurry up and move away from the door.

Taking a quick look around to see if anyone else was nearby, Shay made her way to the alley and stepped into the shadows. "Didn't you find the key I left for you at the front desk?" she asked.

"Does anyone else know you're in town?" Clint asked.

Shay's thoughts drifted back to the dozen or so conversations she'd had with as many people since she'd reacquainted herself with Split Creek. She then looked at the expression on Clint's face to try and guess on whether or not seeing all those people was supposed to be a good or bad thing.

"Maybe a few," was the final answer she settled upon.

"Did you see any of Barstow's men?"

At that moment, Shay noticed the old man standing behind Clint. He had his back to her at first, but when he turned around, Ellis visibly brightened at the sight of her.

"Miss Parkett," Ellis said. "I was hoping nobody got to you yet."

"Good to see you, too," she replied. Turning to Clint, she added, "Ellis is a regular at The Busted Flush."

Clint was still busy making sure that no more gunmen were storming down the street. When he pulled his head back into the alley, he rolled his eyes and let out a heavy sigh. "Well, I'm so glad we all know each other here. Now are you two about ready to go, or is there some more catching up to do?"

Shay gave him a look that reminded Clint of all the snow he'd so recently left behind. Suddenly, he felt like a child who had just used the wrong tone of voice when addressing the teacher.

"There's no reason to be like that," she scolded. "What are you two doing in this alley, anyway?"

"You never answered my question. Did you see any of Barstow's men while you were around town?"

"A few, but they're all over the place. Why?"

"What about the sheriff?"

She nodded and hooked her thumb toward the side of the hotel. "I just saw him rush inside." Turning toward the mouth of the alley, Shay started walking toward the hotel's front door. "I'll bet he's still there if you want to—"

"No," Clint said as he put a hand on her shoulder to keep her from taking another step. "After what happened in Modillo, I'm not too confident about the law around here. And after what just happened in there, I don't think the sheriff will want to be too friendly with me, either."

"Why?" Shay asked. "What happened?"

"We just killed another one of Barstow's men."

Ellis poked his head around Clint and nodded. "It was Ed Laskin."

Clint was becoming more and more frustrated as the conversation progressed. "Look, I don't care anymore who knows who or what any of these killers' names are. Right now, we just need to get the hell out of here and find somewhere else to hole up. We need to get moving quickly and we'd best be damn quiet about it."

Both Ellis and Shay looked at Clint as if he'd just bared his teeth and snarled at them.

Shay then reached out to put a hand on Clint's shoulder. Patting him gently, she said, "No need to get too excited . . ." Seeing the murderous look brewing in Clint's eyes, Shay forced the smile off her face and pointed toward the other end of the alley. "Through there. I know a couple who will put us all up for tonight at least. They owe me a favor and have no love for Barstow."

Clint turned and headed down the alley as the sound of pounding footsteps came from the hotel's narrow staircase.

The door swung outward, blocking his view of Shay and all but a sliver of Ellis.

"Where'd he go?" came a voice from the other side of the door.

Although Clint couldn't see who was doing the talking, he recognized the mixture of aggression and authority in the man's voice that was enough to mark him as one of the town's law.

Clint heard Shay's voice saying something in a hurried, almost sobbing tone. At that moment, Ellis peeked around the door just enough for Clint to notice and waved him on with a quick hand motion.

"I heard the shots," Shay said. "Then someone came out and nearly knocked me down to get to the street."

"He did knock me down," Ellis chimed in. "Took off that way."

Clint didn't like the idea of running from the law, but so far the towns under Barstow's control didn't have much law anyway. Taking his steps nice and easy, Clint backed away from the door and tried not to make a noise that would make the sheriff look his way.

TWENTY-FOUR

"Someone said they saw another person with him," the sheriff said.

When Furlan mentioned that, the lawman started to move off the step leading to the alley so he could get a better look outside. Shay felt her heart jump into the back of her throat when that happened and she knew that Clint hadn't had enough time to get himself properly hidden.

"Wait a second," she said as she whipped around to look at something across the street. Pointing her finger in the opposite direction than the alley, she asked, "Is that the man you're looking for?"

Furlan was a burly man who nearly filled up every bit of the doorway leading from the hotel's stairwell. His short-cropped dark brown hair looked more like fur than anything normally found on top of a man's head. He moved like a wary animal as he stepped forward and hopped down off of the last step to land squarely on both feet. His eyes went from Shay to the street and then his body started turning completely around.

Shay knew the sheriff could see around the door from where he now stood and would be looking back toward Clint within seconds. As much as she wanted to glance back and warn Clint, she knew that that would only look more suspicious and draw more attention to his escape.

"I don't see what you're talking about," Sheriff Furlan said as he turned toward Shay. "Unless you're talking about that man right there."

Shay's stomach dropped down to her toes as Furlan lifted a thick finger to point down into the alley. Trying not to look too panicked, she turned and glanced in the direction he'd indicated. "No," she said once she got a look at Clint's back just before he rounded the other end of the alley. "The man I saw was wearing a coat and was running pretty fast. He's got to be farther away than that."

"I guess you're right," Furlan said grudgingly. He then turned back toward Shay and tipped his hat. "Better stay inside until I catch that one. He's a killer, you know."

Doing a good job of looking rattled, Shay wrapped her arms around herself and drew her shoulders up. She nodded meekly and stepped aside to let the sheriff walk past her toward the street. Once he was gone, she let out a deep breath and tried not to start shaking for real.

"That was close," Ellis said once the sheriff was out of earshot.

But Shay was already walking down the alley. Once she got halfway down the narrow passage, she broke into a run until she came out on the other side. At first, she couldn't see anything but the back end of the hotel and the entrance to another alley leading between neighboring buildings.

"Clint?" she whispered.

Once again, she looked around, but didn't see anything besides the other buildings. Just as she turned to walk along the rear of the hotel, a hand shot out from behind a stack of wooden crates to push solidly against her mouth.

She had just taken in a sharp breath and was about to let it out in the form of a desperate scream when she saw Clint step out and put a finger to his lips.

"Is there anyone coming after you?" he asked as he took his other hand away from her mouth.

Shay pressed a hand against her thumping heart and shook her head. "No. Just Ellis. The sheriff moved on into the street, but he might swing back this way."

Already, Clint was turning to leave. "Well, he won't find much of anything because after I finish up what I was trying to do in my hotel room, we'll be on the move again."

Another set of footsteps came from the alley. Clint's first impulse was to go for his gun, even though he knew who it was that would probably be emerging from the narrow passageway. Sure enough, Ellis came dashing forward. As soon as he saw the look in Clint's eye, he raised his hands and came to a stop.

"Furlan's talkin' to some folks outside the hotel," Ellis said between wheezing breaths. "They're probably telling him that the only one to come outta that alley was him."

"You mentioned those friends of yours who might put us up," Clint said. "Are you sure we can trust them?"

"Enough to keep their mouths shut for a few hours, anyway."

"Good. Let's go."

Even though he wanted to get inside and out of sight as soon as possible, Clint kept his pace slow and easy. If the sheriff or anyone else happened to spot them before they got to where they were going, running would only make Clint and the rest stick out more in those people's minds.

Besides, even if Barstow was in an entirely different town, Clint wasn't about to give him the satisfaction of seeing him run away twice in one day.

TWENTY-FIVE

"We're going after him."

The words struck Deputy Rivera like a cold slap in the face. He looked away from the man who'd said them and wanted to keep his mouth shut. But the more he tried to hold it back, the more the response bubbled up inside of him until it made his guts twist into a burning knot.

"Are you serious?" Rivera finally asked.

Barstow had been sitting in relative silence with his feet propped up on what used to be the sheriff's desk. He sat there content in the knowledge that he owned the office as well as the man who had taken it over. In fact, he'd owned all those things for quite some time.

"It's not your place to ask me that," Barstow said. "All you need to do is ask me how you think we should do it."

"But Adams already left town. Everyone saw him go. Why chase him down when you've been so . . ." The deputy bit his tongue before finishing that last part.

Barstow had been sitting with his fingers steepled and his eyes locked onto a point in space directly in front of him. Ever since Tannen and the others had returned from their ride, Modillo had felt more quiet than ever before. It had the air of a military cemetery during the middle of a war. It might have been calm compared to the rest of the turmoil going on around it, but there was death hanging in the slowly churning breeze.

103

And there was the promise of more to come.

"You ever been to Ander's Valley?" Barstow asked just before the silence got too uncomfortable.

Ander's Valley was a town that formed a triangle in the area along with Modillo and Split Creek. The place wasn't as big as the other two, but it was growing due to its proximity to Santa Fe. There were plenty of stages that went through there, which meant a lot of opportunities for saloon owners and gamblers. More recently, there had been rumors of scouts from the Union Pacific poking their noses around that area, which would mean even bigger things for the Valley's future.

"I been there once," Rivera replied. "Wasn't much more than a wide spot in the road."

"How long ago was that?"

"Few years."

"Well, the place has grown up since then. And from what I hear, it's set to grow even more in years to come. I want you to head out there and meet up with their law. Keep your eyes open so you can tell me how ripe they are for the picking."

Rivera's eyes widened. "You want to move into Ander's Valley?"

"Now's the time to do it. If we wait any longer, the place might be too much trouble or too well protected by more . . . legitimate interests."

"And what does that have to do with going after Adams?"

Barstow took a moment to fish inside his vest pocket for a fresh cigar. After pulling a stogie out and running it under his nose, he chewed off the end of it like a wolf gnawing on a bone. He then spit the stub out of his mouth and struck a match against the edge of the bar. "I was just getting to that," he said while touching the flame to the end of the cigar.

Puffing in a few breaths of smoke, Barstow said, "I'm not all that sure on why Adams chose to leave. If he's half of what his reputation says he is, he probably felt this town was just a little more trouble than it was worth. And you know what I think about that?"

Barstow let the question hang in the air right alongside the cloud of smoke that grew around his head. "I think he's right."

The front door to the saloon opened to let in a pair of locals arriving for one of the poker games in the back of the room. The Busted Flush had been filling up steadily throughout the day, but that was nothing special. Barstow and Rivera had been planted at or around the bar for most of that time, which was nothing special either. The only thing that made this day stand out from all the others was the amount of times men had come into the place just to have a word or two with the saloon's well-dressed owner.

One such man came in behind the two gamblers and walked right up to Barstow, leaned in to his ear and whispered a few sentences. Barstow nodded and shooed the man away.

Rivera knew better than to ask about Barstow's business. Most of the time he found he was better off not knowing about it anyway. "If this town is so much trouble, then why don't you move on to somewhere else?" the deputy asked.

"I said this place was more trouble than it was worth. That doesn't mean it's not worth having. Hell, boy, I can handle a lot more trouble than what this place has to offer. But I don't just have to worry about this town. There's also Split Creek. Even so, that's such a shithole that it's more of a headache than Modillo.

"Both those towns together have made for a pretty good business, though. Still, I'd be better off running a few high-stakes casinos in San Francisco or New York." Barstow paused to enjoy his cigar, rolling it between thumb and forefinger while savoring the confused look on Rivera's face. "But let me tell you something," he finally said. "*Three* towns . . . now that would be worth any amount of trouble."

Rivera shook his head as though he'd just been told about his own death. "And Adams?"

"Killing Adams is just the sort of thing to ease our way into Ander's Valley and tighten my hold on this entire part of the state. The marshals don't do much more than pass through these parts and most of the local laws are in my pocket already."

Turning his head slightly, Rivera cringed when he heard that last statement. He looked as though he wanted to dispute it, but knew that he had nothing to say in his own defense.

With the cigar clamped between his teeth, Barstow rolled on in his speech as though he was already marching across New Mexico. "We'll kill Adams nice and messy in a public place. Word'll spread like a spark through dry leaves and by the time we step anywhere in this state, we'll be known as the ones who took down a legend. Once we get the people scared, the rest is gravy."

Another set of gamblers swaggered into the saloon with money in their pockets and smiles upon their faces. That would change within a matter of hours or possibly even minutes when they would be slinking out to explain their losses to whoever waited for them at home. Rivera looked over to them and remembered when he'd worked with the sheriff as a real lawman. Back in those days, he might have kept an eye on the fathers and husbands in that saloon to make sure they didn't lose more than they could afford. It was a part of taking care of the people in Modillo. Now, he concerned himself with putting the fear of god into those same people and taking advantage of the openings they created when they squirmed.

"What's the matter, Rivera?" Barstow asked. "You look like you're not too happy about my proposal."

"I'm not sure if it'll be all that easy to walk in and take over another town. Split Creek was easy because it was small enough and it took a lot of spilled blood to get where you are here. Wouldn't a move to Ander's Valley be spreading yourself a little thin?"

"That's why we're not gonna move into that place like we did the others." Leaning in with his elbow on the bar, Barstow lowered his voice to a grating whisper. "Adams is in Split Creek now and already he's been forced to shoot a man dead."

"What?"

"You know those men that came through here? They've been feeding me reports from the wire. I just heard about the shooting a few minutes ago and it won't be the last. A reputation can only go so far in the face of facts, and as the bodies start piling up, the people will see Adams for what he is . . . a cold-blooded killer."

"But he isn't—"

"Of course he ain't, but not everyone knows that."

"And how do you know he'll kill anyone else?"

"I know because they're my men," Barstow said as he inhaled the noxious smoke from his cigar. The end of it glowed like a demon's eye and he flicked a chunk of ash to the floor. "My men will go where I tell them to go and they'll fight who I tell them to fight. The only tricky part will be herding my killer into Ander's Valley. Once he's there, we sweep in and rid this land of a murderous criminal."

Barstow got a faraway look in his eyes and little tendrils of smoke curled out of his nostrils. "A legend . . . fallen from grace."

TWENTY-SIX

The people that owed Shay a favor were a young couple who had been married less than a year and a half earlier. The man's name was Paul; he was a bulky redhead with a broken nose and arms laden with thick layers of muscle. He was married to a short woman named Sarah who had fine, light brown hair and a smile that was bright enough to light up the room even when Shay brought two complete strangers into her house.

After a quick bit of explaining, Sarah filled her arms with linens and busied herself with the task of fixing up a spare bed in the next room. Paul kept his eyes on Clint and Ellis, obviously not quite sure of what he thought of them yet.

"Shay tells me you all got into some trouble," Paul said.

Ellis nodded solemnly. "Afraid so. We're on the run from some men who want us dead."

"Why do these men want you dead?"

"Because we survived the last time they tried to kill us."

Paul thought about that for a second and a half before breaking out into bellowing laughter. "Now that's one helluva reason if I ever heard one," he said, slapping the older man on the back. "Your name's Ellis, right?"

"You got it."

As soon as Paul shook hands with the old man and looked over to the next person in line, Clint extended his own hand and introduced himself.

"Clint Adams?" Paul asked. His voice was tinged with equal parts doubt and reverence.

"That's what I said. I sure appreciate what you're doing for us. Don't worry, though, because we won't impose on you for very long."

Paul shook his head. "Forget about it. Stay as long as you like. I may be a quiet sort, but I don't mind giving Barstow a hard time whenever I can get away with it."

"Shay told you that Barstow was the one after us?"

"She didn't have to. If there's some gunmen after someone around here, the smart money's riding on the fact that it's Barstow behind it. So what did you do to get him all riled up?"

Clint pulled up a chair and sat down. It felt good to be inside a home rather than a hotel or the trail. Even though it wasn't his, the place was tidy and comfortable. It was almost enough to let Clint put his guard down. Almost, but not quite.

"I called him out for cheating at cards," Clint said.

Once again, Paul broke out into laughter and slapped Ellis on the back. The old man seemed to be enjoying himself, but didn't appreciate the extra attention.

"Sorry, Ellis, but a man doesn't just roughhouse with someone like Clint Adams. I heard he's even faster than Billy the Kid."

"I don't know about that," Clint said. "But I know I've got a better temper."

This time, when the fits of laughter rippled through his body, Paul let them run their course as they shook him from head to toe. By the time they got to his upper body, Paul's arm straightened out, reared back his hand and let it fly until the redhead's palm swatted against Clint's back.

Once the man's laughter died down a bit, Paul said, "It's about damn time that somebody held that slimy son of a bitch accountable for his actions. I just wish I could've been there to see the look on his face when you did it."

Right about this time, Clint remembered the look that Paul was talking about and it did actually strike him as funny. "If you've ever been fishing and saw the expression a trout gets right about when it gets plucked from the river and thrown onto dry land for the first time, that'd be about what he looked like."

"Well that would certainly explain why life's been so hard the last few days."

"What do you mean?"

The expression on Paul's face changed from laughter to reflection in a way that reminded Clint of an iceberg melting away as the weather got warmer. "I mean that the men working for him have been asking about you since yesterday night and they haven't been too happy with any kind of answer besides the one that ends up with them getting any closer to getting their hands on you.

"I've seen when Barstow is after somebody, Mister Adams. He rattles his chains and hollers until that someone winds up delivered to his door. But I ain't never seen him get as worked up as he is now. Whatever his reasons, he seems to want to get a hold of you pretty badly. Just because you're here for now, that doesn't mean I can protect you for very long."

All of the humor had run dry from Ellis's smile. It left him looking hollow and uncomfortable as he thought about what Paul was saying. The old man turned toward Clint and nodded his head. "It can get pretty bad when Barstow wants it to. That's what I wanted to tell you when I tracked you down the first time. No matter how hard you try, there just ain't no hiding from the man who can turn the screws on an entire town."

"All I need is a few hours," Clint said. "Just enough time to finish some work that I started. Once I'm done, it'll be time for me to take the offensive."

Paul looked as though he desperately wanted to take some comfort from Clint's words, but couldn't quite muster up the faith required for the task. "You're welcome to stay, but most folks around here would tell Barstow's men what they want to know just out of sheer instinct. They ain't bad people, you understand. They just don't know anything else besides what Barstow tells them."

Before Clint could ask any other questions, they were interrupted by Shay and Sarah coming back into the room with pleasant smiles on their faces. They'd been talking about something or other that had left them in rather high spirits. Clint got the impression that life in Split Creek and Modillo was a lot like that; a lot of fear broken up by whatever happiness could flourish if you didn't look too hard at your circumstances. It was similar to living in a war zone. The battles didn't seem as bad if you just didn't spend your days watching them too closely.

"You've got your few hours," Paul said calmly. "If you can stay quiet and lay low, you're more than welcome to stay the night. But Barstow's men will track you down eventually. There ain't nothing you can do to prevent that."

"That's no way to talk to our guests, Paul," Sarah scolded. "They can stay for as long as they want. Nobody deserves to be handed over to that animal."

Shay put a calm hand on the other woman's shoulder. "We really appreciate it."

Paul glanced over to his wife, but focused right back on Clint. "Things in these parts aren't all that bad. Not so long as Barstow keeps happy. And I can already tell by the way his men are stomping through here all of a sudden that he ain't all too happy."

"I meant what I said about only staying for a very short time. We'll be out of here before anyone's had a chance to figure out where we've been. And after that, I'm not too worried about Barstow's men tracking me down," Clint said. "In fact, I'm counting on it."

TWENTY-SEVEN

There was a social being held at the church and Paul and Sarah had left to put in their appearance. Actually, Clint insisted on them going. If push came to shove and they were found in the couple's home, Clint, Shay and Ellis would say that they'd broken into the place so Paul and Sarah wouldn't get hurt for being kind to strangers.

Ellis found a rocker in the corner of the couple's bedroom where he could collapse for a while. Clint sat at the table in the dining room with his borrowed tools and gun parts once again laid out in front of him. This time when he worked, he felt none of the joy he had earlier. His fingers were just as nimble, but his mind was anything but relaxed by the routine.

He worked because he needed to. Time was of the essence and if he didn't make all the proper adjustments to the Colt, his life would be put in danger. Not that he was worried about making a mistake. He knew his craft too well for those kind of concerns. Rather, he was worried about the way things had been shaping up with Barstow.

The more he heard about that man, the more Clint realized what a problem he was. At first, he'd been convinced that Barstow was nothing more than a powerful bully who muscled his way into power and held onto it through brute force. The man was definitely all of that, but there was something else beneath the surface. Something more troubling.

Besides having men and guns on his side, Barstow had been able to get the people of his towns to go along with him, however grudgingly, which made saving them all the more difficult. For all Clint knew, Barstow had been able to keep track of him through the help of the very folks he'd been fighting for.

In fact, at this very moment, Paul and Sarah could be talking to Barstow's men. . . .

"What are you up to?" Shay asked, interrupting Clint's uneasy thoughts.

Clint looked down at what he'd been doing and saw that he was just about to fit the newly re-tooled cylinder into his Colt. Shaking the distractions out of his mind, he looked down at the pistol and snapped the piece into place. It fit perfectly with a sharp, subdued *click*.

"Just finishing up work on my Colt," he said. "Looks like I'll be able to save it after all."

Shay looked down at the gun in his hands and ran her fingers over the well-oiled metal. Even though she was no expert, she was impressed with the way one piece fit snugly against the other as though the entire mechanism was a single part. She sat down next to him and moved her hand down over the barrel, then across the cylinder to the handle and finally onto his knuckles and the back of his hand.

"I always thought they called you the Gunsmith because of how you shot them," she said. "I didn't know you actually fixed them as well."

Clint turned his attention to one of the spare guns he'd picked up and began stripping it for the few remaining parts he needed for the Colt's firing mechanism. "Actually, I've made a decent living at fixing them."

"Somehow I can't really see you as a craftsman."

"Really? Why not?"

Moving in closer to him, Shay ran her hands over Clint's. She caressed his fingers and then gently brushed her fingertips over his arms. "Don't get me wrong. I already know how good you are with your hands. It's just that I have a hard time picturing you in such a quiet life."

Thinking back to the days before he'd made a name for

himself, Clint was struck by just how long ago it seemed that he used to travel in his wagon and get paid for every little job he took on. The more he thought about it, the more he missed that old wagon, which now sat in West Texas. "I don't have any trouble picturing a quieter life," he said. "Actually, I miss it."

Shay's hands were still wandering over Clint's body, moving along his shoulders until they worked their way up his neck. When her fingers ran through his hair, she turned his head to face her and leaned in for a slow, passionate kiss.

TWENTY-EIGHT

Her lips felt warm and soft against Clint's own, tasting slightly of wild berries. When he gave in and kissed her back, Shay moaned from the back of her throat in a way that sent little ripples through her lips and onto Clint's skin. She held him in her hands as though she was afraid of him trying to get away. Clint wanted no such thing, however, and dropped his tools onto the table so he could explore the generous curves of her body.

As he moved his hands over her waist and then up along her sides, Shay leaned her head back and smiled. "That's so nice," she purred. "You definitely have the touch of a man who knows how to use his hands."

She wore a simple dress that fit tightly against her body. Wherever he placed his hands, Clint could feel her body moving here and there until he'd managed to touch her every place he could possibly reach. The fabric of her clothing cinched her breasts in and when he rubbed his palms over them, she arched her back and moaned slightly. He could feel her nipples hardening through the material and when he moved one hand down to cup her bottom, Shay swung one leg over him and moved sideways so she could straddle him where he sat.

"You know Ellis is in the next room," Clint said even as he slid his hand beneath her skirts and pulled her in closer.

Shay looked over toward the closed door and then went

115

back to nibbling on Clint's ear. "I'd rather not think about him," she said. "I'd rather spend all my thoughts on you and you alone."

He now had both hands under her dress and was savoring the smooth texture of her skin and the way her muscles tensed and writhed as she tightened her legs around him and strained to rub against the growing bulge in his pants. Her own hands moved down low to feverishly work at the buckle on his belt and when she pulled it free, she all but tore his jeans off of him.

Clint could feel the soft layers of underclothing beneath Shay's dress. The material was heated by her skin and when he felt between her legs, he knew for sure just how much she wanted him.

Shay had already worked his cock out of his clothing and was stroking its length with one hand. She used the other hand to reach down and pull up her skirts so she could climb up onto him until she was poised over the head of his cock.

Clint leaned back slightly and grabbed hold of the flimsy material separating him from the moist patch between Shay's legs. With one quick pull, the fabric tore in half and was tossed aside to the floor. Looking down into his eyes with a wild, hungry smile on her face, Shay moved her hips in little circles, gently teasing him by brushing the lips of her vagina over his rigid pole.

"You trying to drive me crazy?" Clint asked as he grabbed her buttocks and pulled her down lower.

Shay flicked her tongue out to wet her lips. With a single motion of her head, she whipped her hair around so that it fell over both of their faces like a fine, golden curtain. "It's only fair," she said. "You've been driving me crazy all day long."

Moving one hand up over her back, Clint pulled her down even closer so he could kiss her fully on the lips. Their tongues probed one another, each tasting the other while their bodies continued to brush together. Clint could feel the soft lips between her legs opening slightly for him as they came together. But rather than sate his desires just yet, he rubbed the length of his shaft over those lips until Shay held him tightly and clenched her eyes shut.

At that moment, Clint thrust his hips upward and plunged his cock deep inside of her, causing Shay to grunt loudly and dig her nails into his skin.

"Oh god, yes," she moaned while lowering herself down onto him.

With her hands wrapped around his neck, Shay braced her knees upon the bench they shared and moved her body up and down while grinding back and forth. She could feel the juices running over her lips and onto Clint's shaft, making the next thrust glide in even easier than the one before.

Clint reached around to pull the dress down from Shay's shoulders until it fell away from her body. Her breasts bounced slightly as she rode on top of him, the small, dark nipples as hard as two pieces of candy. Leaning back, Shay reclined in his arms and let the sensations flow through her entire body. Even through the bundled material, Clint could see the way her stomach rose and fell in time to their thrusting bodies.

Grabbing her tightly, Clint lifted her right along with him as he stood up and pushed the bench away behind him. Shay's face lit up as she felt herself getting lifted into the air and she grabbed hold of him that much tighter.

"You found your second wind, I see," she giggled while clenching her legs around him.

"I may have been distracted by a little matter of trying not to get killed and staying away from the gunmen out to shoot me down, but I'm not blind. You have no idea how hard it is to keep my hands off of you whenever I think about the last time we did this."

Shay leaned back and swept aside the tools and gun parts with a wave of her arm. Before she lost her balance, she quickly locked her hands behind Clint's neck and shifted her hips. He was still inside of her and when he stood up, the base of his penis rubbed just right against a spot on her body that sent shivers up her spine. "Then let's make some new memories so we can both be distracted later on."

Just as Clint was about to set her down on the edge of the

table, Shay ground her hips against him until he fit tightly inside of her. He knew exactly what she wanted and was more than happy to give it to her.

Straightening his back, Clint gripped her buttocks with both hands and supported her weight as she began bouncing in his arms. She rode him while standing up for as long as he could hold her until she finally began to slow down, her breath becoming more ragged against his neck.

Leaning forward just enough to set her down onto the table, Clint stepped back to get a look at her. Shay propped herself up with her arms behind her and looked into Clint's eyes with raw, carnal desire. With her heels resting on the edge of the bench, she spread her legs open wide, offering him the slick pink lips in between her thighs.

Clint stepped up and ran his hands along the inside of her legs. She trembled slightly as his fingers brushed over her vagina and then slipped inside. He used those same fingers to trace a line up over her stomach as he bent down to place his mouth against the little nub of flesh over her opening.

Shay's knuckles turned white as she gripped onto the edge of the table. Her breath caught in her throat as wave after wave of pleasure wracked every muscle in her body with sharp convulsions. Letting herself fall back onto the table, she grabbed hold of the back of Clint's head and thrust her hips closer to his mouth.

When her grip relaxed on him, Clint stood back up and fit his penis between her legs. He thrust into her just hard enough to rock the table back an inch or so, but Shay didn't seem to mind. She just held on and chewed on her lower lip to prevent herself from screaming out at the top of her voice.

Clint could feel the approaching climax and grabbed hold of her hips with both hands so he could thrust into her even harder. He could feel Shay's legs wrap around him and squeeze him tightly as she tossed her hair from side to side. When she arched her back, she pushed her rigid little nipples into the air and began pounding her fist against the table as another orgasm shot set every one of her nerve endings on fire.

By the time Clint noticed the layer of sweat covering

Shay's skin, he was exploding inside of her with a pleasure so intense that it made it difficult for him to keep his feet beneath him. Once the passion had subsided, he was the one gripping the edge of the table before allowing himself to drop heavily onto the bench.

"Good lord," he rasped while wiping at his forehead with the back of his hand.

Shay reclined on the table and ran her fingers lazily through her hair. As her smile grew into a tempting smirk, her fingers traced over her breasts and around the nipples before rubbing gently along her stomach. "Now that's what I call a distraction."

Just then, the sound of footsteps came from the other room, followed by Ellis's coughing and grumbling sleepily to himself. Shay was barely able to hold back her laughter as she quickly pulled her dress back into place and started picking up the things she'd thrown to the floor. Clint, too, rushed into his clothes and pulled the table back into its original place.

The door to the bedroom came open to reveal Ellis's tired face. "What happened out here?" he asked once he saw the mess.

"Nothing," Shay replied while gathering up the tools. "Clint just sat me up on that table and had his way with me."

"Fine," Ellis mumbled. "If you don't want to tell me, you don't need to be smart about it."

TWENTY-NINE

Sheriff Furlan stood in the doorway to the telegraph office with his hands on his hips. The glare he gave to the little man behind the desk was so intense that the teller had to hunch his shoulders and lower his eyes rather than try to look the lawman in the face. It had only been a minute or two since Furlan had walked into the small building, but there was enough tension in the air to fill an entire day.

Finally, the black contraption connected to the wire, which came in through a hole in the ceiling, began twitching and giving off a series of erratic ticks. In a flash, the teller was next to the machine with a pencil and paper in hand. He responded to the alert with a few ticks of his own and then waited for the message to come through. Once he started writing, the sheriff loomed behind him like an imposing shadow.

"That from him?" Furlan asked.

The teller nodded, trying not to be distracted from the rattling signal that flooded in over the wire.

After a while, the ticking stopped and the teller sent one last confirmation signal. The little man held out the paper and pulled his hand back once the telegram was snatched away from him.

Furlan read it with a stern look on his face and then looked up at the teller. "Did you read any of this?" he asked.

The teller looked stumped for a second and then nodded

meekly. "I . . . I kind of had to. But whatever comes across the wire is strictly kept between myself and the person to whom the message is sent."

Although he didn't have to, Furlan read through the message again and turned to leave. He was an imposing figure out in the open, but within the confines of the little office, he looked even larger and more intimidating. He'd never given the teller a reason to fear him. Rather, it was just the natural response similar to the way a field mouse ran from the cat.

"You'd be smart to forget about what you read," Furlan stated in an even tone. "If anyone asks, you never even received this message. Understand?"

"Yessir, Sheriff."

Turning to leave, Furlan folded up the paper and stuck it into his shirt pocket. Before he could open the door, he was stopped by a timid question coming from the field mouse sitting next to the telegraph.

"Sheriff?"

Furlan kept the door shut, but didn't turn around. "What's on your mind?"

"What it says in that cable . . . is it true?"

The sheriff's first impulse was to keep walking and let the door shut behind him. But then he thought about the contents of the telegram and what it could mean for the people of Split Creek. "Yeah," he said finally. "I'm afraid it is."

"I won't tell no one," the smaller man said. "I just wanted to know if I should keep my head down for a while. Maybe stay inside away from the streets."

Furlan opened the door and stepped outside. Turning to look over his shoulder, he looked inside the office and said, "That might not be such a bad idea."

The streets of Split Creek were not as busy as those in Modillo, but there were enough people around to keep the town awake after the sun went down. There were only two saloons and a billiard room, which were all clumped together on the edge of town facing the road to Santa Fe.

The biggest of those saloons was called Kyle's Spirit

House and was run by an Englishman who'd come to the States to find his fortune. Unfortunately, he never found much of anything outside of the town limits, but that didn't keep him from putting together a saloon that was one of the best in the area.

Sheriff Furlan walked straight from the telegraph office to Kyle's, ignoring all the tipped hats and friendly greetings along the way. Much like the little teller he'd left behind, most of the people in town were more than a little intimidated by their sheriff. But as long as they didn't spend too much time with him, they seemed happy with their choice. After all, as long as the muscular figure was on their side, they didn't mind giving him his space.

Rounding the corner that put him on the same street as Kyle's, Furlan immediately spotted a pair of men walking straight for him. He might have been startled if he hadn't been expecting to find them there in the first place. Even with the distance between them and the fading sunlight, Furlan could spot Tannen's beady eyes and dark-stained teeth more than half a block away. The man beside Tannen was another of Barstow's killers and not of much concern to Furlan.

The three men walked straight for each other and met in front of a closed feed store two doors away from Kyle's.

"I just got word from your boss," Furlan said as he pulled the scrap of paper from his pocket and held it in front of him. "There's no reason for this. I can track this man down on my own. I don't need your help."

"It ain't about what you need," Tannen sneered. "It's about what *we* need. And what we need is to find Adams and flush him out before he gets too comfortable. If we don't work together, he might just slip out of here and head in the wrong direction."

"He won't get out of town. I posted my deputies on watch after we found the body in the hotel. When we find him, I'll deal with him like I would any man accused of murder."

Tannen glared up at the lawman. Although Furlan outweighed him by at least fifty pounds and stood about half a foot taller, Tannen looked as though he was about to spit into the sheriff's eye. He reached out and snatched the paper from Furlan's hand and read it over.

"I don't know about you," Tannen said. "But I see this as an order coming from Barstow himself." He then turned the paper around and shoved it up close to the lawman's face. "Why don't you read it for me?"

It was obvious that Furlan was trying to rein in his temper. His eyes narrowed to fiery slits and his nostrils flared like a bull's. "Tannen, I'm warning you. Back off or I swear I'll—"

"You'll *what*?"

Furlan took a deep breath as both his hands settled onto the guns strapped into the double rig around his waist. He knew he could kill both of these men without too much trouble. But there would be others that would come after him . . . and then others after that. From what he'd heard, Barstow had a small army at his disposal between Split Creek and Modillo. It was those countless others that kept the sheriff in check.

"Why don't you read that to me?" Tannen prodded, flaunting his edge over the lawman with a filthy grin.

"I know what it says."

"Read it."

Furlan stared at Tannen with a look that would have melted any other man quicker than icicle on a summer day. When he spoke, his words were just as cold and just as sharp. "It says: 'Tear town apart until Adams is found. Kill those with him if necessary. Send him to Ander's Valley.' "

"There," Tannen said as he pulled the paper back and folded it neatly. "That wasn't so hard."

The sheriff's fist swung up like a delivery straight from hell. When it impacted against Tannen's jaw, it lifted the wiry man onto his toes and dropped him onto his ass. The man next to Tannen started toward Furlan, but stopped the moment he saw the gun in the lawman's hand along with the threat in his eyes.

"If Barstow wants blood to run in my streets, then that's the way it'll be whether I like it or not," Furlan said. "But if you don't watch yourself, the first blood that's gonna be spilled will be yours."

Rubbing his jaw, Tannen got to his feet and spit a red glob onto the dirt. "There's yer blood. Now are you gonna be a good little doggie and do as yer told, or do I have to take this further?"

Looking down at the other man, Furlan actually started to laugh. "I'm not the one you have to worry about, Tannen."

THIRTY

The Colt spun around Clint's finger like a flicker of silvery light. With a twist of his wrist, the pistol changed direction and spun the other way until it stopped dead in his grasp. Clint sighted down the barrel with a careful eye and rolled the cylinder against his palm.

Ellis and Shay watched from the other side of the room. They'd left him alone after he insisted on getting some peace and quiet so he could finally put his task to rest. Now, with all the tools wrapped in the oilcloth and the other two guns laying in pieces on the table, Clint stood and slid the Colt into its familiar space at his side.

He then turned and drew the gun in a motion that was so fast, it caused both of the people watching him to jump back.

"If you're trying to impress us," Shay said, "it worked."

Holding the gun sideways and pulling the hammer back with his thumb, Clint said, "This isn't exactly for show." Satisfied with the smooth action of the hammer and the perfect turning of the cylinder, Clint spun the pistol in his hand quick enough for it to make a whirling sound as it cut through the air. The Colt whirled perfectly about his torso and hip like a metal hummingbird circling his holster. When he slapped the pistol back into its holster, Clint held his hands out palms down and shook his fingers as though he'd burned them.

"All right," he said. "Maybe that part was for show."

Just as the smile worked its way onto Clint's face, the front door to the little house burst open and Sarah came running inside. Her skin was pale and there were tears streaming from the corners of her eyes. Her breath came in deep, gasping bursts that shook her entire body.

"My god," Shay said as she rushed over to put her arms around the smaller woman. "What on earth happened?"

"You've got to get out of here," she said in between sobs. "You've got to take your things and leave right now. Right this instant!"

Ellis was frozen in his place and he looked toward Clint for direction. When Clint nodded and pointed toward the little pile of their belongings, the old man stooped down to begin collecting them.

Clint walked over to Sarah and looked into her eyes. "What's the matter? Did somebody come after you?"

Just then, the door opened again and it was Paul standing on the front step. For a second, he just looked inside at his wife. "You better do what she says," he told everyone else. "And you'd best do it quick."

When Clint looked over at him, Paul turned to stare intently back at him. There was an urgency in his gaze that hung heavily in the air between them like a silent scream held back by a killer's smothering hand.

Instinctually, Clint reached for the Colt as Paul began stepping to one side. With the other man still in the way, however, he kept himself from drawing even as he saw one of Tannen's men standing on the porch.

"I'm sorry, Clint," Paul said as he hung his head low and stood aside so the man behind him could walk into the house.

The gunman was careful to put himself as close to Ellis and Sarah as possible since those were the two closest to his side of the door. Even though he wore the smug look of someone confident in his superiority, he still kept clear of both Clint and Paul. As soon as he let the door swing closed, he raised his hand and leveled a gun at Clint.

The door swung toward the jamb, but stopped short as it was caught by a gloved hand. When it swung inside yet again, another pair of gunmen walked inside. One of them carried a sawed-off shotgun while the other held a .45 pistol at hip level. They all lined up in front of Clint and the others like a makeshift firing squad.

For a second, Clint thought they were going to start shooting without saying a word. They all looked toward the women and old man as though they were trying to imagine what their helpless screams would sound like. But when they turned to face Clint and Paul, the vicious gleam in their eyes disappeared and they took up more defensive postures.

"So you're Clint Adams?" asked the man who'd been the first to walk in behind Paul. "We've been hearing a whole lot about you."

Clint stood tall and didn't allow the slightest trace of worry to drift onto his face. "Where's Tannen?"

Ignoring Clint's question, the gunman looked about the room and went to the bedroom door. After pushing it open and checking inside, he pulled the door closed again until it shut tightly into place. Satisfied that he could see everyone inside the little house, he turned once again to Clint. "This just doesn't seem like your style. From what I hear, you're some kind of devil with a gun in your hand and we find you hiding in somebody's kitchen."

"Everyone's got to eat," Clint said dryly.

"Not everyone. Not after they been buried six feet under."

The rest of his men seemed to find that amusing and began laughing.

Clint laughed a little, too, as he scanned the faces of each man in turn. With nothing more than quick glances, he decided who would be more likely to shoot first or who might not want to be here at all. A small trick picked up after years at more poker tables than he could rightly remember, the search for tells had saved his life more than once. It might not have showed him much, but a little was all he'd ever needed.

From what he could see, the man with the .45 would more than likely follow any order he was given. He looked ready to jump and he laughed a little too hard at the leader's joke. It seemed like he was trying hard to please the other man.

The guy with the shotgun, however, seemed a little more

reserved. His eyes shifted nervously between every person in the room and he clutched his weapon without any of the familiarity an experienced killer would show with his tool of choice. Actually, Clint would have bet that that shotgun was thrust into his hands at the last minute. It was the kind of gun that didn't require a lot of skill or courage. If the shooter could just pull the trigger once and have it pointed in the correct general direction, the job would be complete.

Clint's assessment of the gunmen took just as long as it would have taken if they were sitting around a poker table: just under twenty seconds or so. With a better handle on who he was dealing with, Clint positioned himself so he could get a clear shot at either the leader of the men or the one with the .45. "So now Barstow wants to improve his nasty reputation by killing women and old men, huh?"

"Nah," the leader said. "He'll improve his reputation by killing you."

"Then let the rest go."

The gunmen actually seemed to consider that for a second. In fact, the man with the shotgun seemed as though he was anxious to clear out the room a bit. But then the leader shook his head and squared off with Clint. Before he locked eyes with him, however, he glanced back to his man with the .45.

If Clint hadn't been watching them all so closely, he might have missed the subtle nod given by the leader to the man with the pistol.

"We can't exactly let you go," the leader said. "None of you. So if you're gonna make a move, do it now."

"But, Will," said the shotgunner. "We're just supposed to—"

"Shut yer mouth!" the leader barked. "I know what we're supposed to do."

Clint kept his eyes on the two gunmen closest to him. The leader and the .45 stood like coiled springs. When the leader motioned back to the .45, Clint was the one to burst into motion as his hand went to the Colt at his side.

By the looks on their faces, all of the gunmen had been taken off guard. The leader seemed especially stunned since he was so confident in the advantage he'd thought he had.

The .45 came up and swung directly toward Shay and Sarah. Clint had been trying to keep the others focused in on him and it took him a split second to redirect his aim. Both of the guns went off at once.

A gout of smoke and sparks blasted from the .45, the sound of which combined with Clint's Colt to create a clap of thunder inside the crowded room.

Pitching backward and tumbling to the floor, the man with the .45 snarled in pain. As he fell, he left a trail of blood, which hung in the air for a moment like the stroke of a gory paintbrush. He landed on the floor in an awkward heap, wrapping both hands around himself to try and keep the blood from pumping out of his chest. But Clint's bullet had done its job too well, and soon the man didn't even have enough strength to hold onto his .45.

Clint turned to make sure the women were all right. What he saw was Shay bent over and reaching out for Sarah who had dropped to the floor and was propped up against the wall.

"Oh god, no!" Paul screamed as he ran straight for his wife.

THIRTY-ONE

Clint was just able to see Paul run toward his wife before he knew the next shot would be coming his way. He turned to look at the leader of the gunmen and saw the other man taking quick aim in his direction. Clint wasted no time in dropping to one knee and swiveling around to put both the leader and the shotgunner in his sights.

The first shot from the leader's gun tore through the space over Clint's head and dug a hole through the back wall. Just as Clint was about to return fire, he saw the shotgun out of the corner of his eye. More specifically, he saw the barrel of the shotgun swinging around toward him. He had just enough time to tuck his body down low and roll forward as the shotgun blast exploded toward him.

Paul's voice thundered through the room like the howl of an angry wolf coming from where he was crouched down in the corner. When he rose up to his feet, he held his hands out in front of him and looked around as though he wasn't quite sure of where he was.

Even from where Clint had landed, he could plainly see the blood covering Paul's hands and smeared across the front of his shirt. The big redhead set his eyes on the shotgunner first and began charging toward him, paying no mind to the weapon in his hands.

Another pistol shot cracked through the air, which bit into the dining room table that stood between Clint and the gunmen's leader. Another shot followed after that and then a third. Each shot crept closer to where Clint was crouching. If there had been a fourth, it would have probably drilled through Clint's flesh.

Before that could happen, however, Clint threw himself forward and twisted onto his side, landing with a painful grunt as his ribs absorbed most of the impact. Even though it sent a dull, thumping pain through his chest and torso, Clint had gotten the effect he'd been after.

Seeing the motion coming from behind the table, the gunmen's leader knew Clint would be breaking cover. He anticipated the other man's movements and fired his last rounds at the level Clint's chest and head would be when he came running out. Since he didn't run out, however, most of the bullets dug into the walls. By the time he saw Clint laying on his side on the floor, the leader was pulling his trigger and about to drop the hammer on his last round.

Clint could feel the bullets whipping over his head. The shooter must have seen him at the last second, because one of the rounds grazed Clint's forearm before burying itself into the nearby wall. The splintered floor scraped through his pants and into his skin as he slid to a stop, but it was worth it for the position he was in.

All Clint could see was the bloodthirsty look on the shooter's face as he pulled his gun down to aim the last bullet he had. Clint moved the Colt up to fire as though he was pointing his finger at his target. At the same time, he squeezed the trigger and pushed forward with his legs. As he threw his body toward the corner, Clint could hear the leader's gun going off one more time and could feel the heat of the bullet passing through the space he'd just left behind. When the twin gunshots faded away, there was a pained grunt and the heavy thump of another body hitting the floor.

Not wanting to be trapped in a bad spot, Clint leapt to his feet and spun around to put his back to the wall and take stock of where the others were in the room. What he saw was a calamity waiting to happen.

*   *   *

Paul stood up with his wife's blood coating his hands and could still see the blank look in her eyes as she'd fallen to the floor. The moment she'd been hit replayed itself over and over in his mind. By the time he'd gotten to her, he knew it was too late. There was nothing left in those eyes. No recognition. No soul. No life.

She was gone.

They'd killed her.

Those two things were all he could think about as he turned toward the closest gunman he could find and began to charge. He saw the shotgun in the man's hands, but couldn't get himself to be too concerned about it. When Paul looked into that man's face, he just wanted to snuff the life out of him . . . make his eyes cold and dead just like poor Sarah's.

Paul's hands fit around the shotgunner's neck with room to spare. As soon as he began to squeeze, Paul could feel the other man struggle. He could feel the breaths trying to make it past his thumbs like frightened little mice trapped in his throat.

The sounds of more gunshots rattled in his ears, but all Paul could care about was crushing the shotgunner's throat and then moving on to the next of the intruders who'd violated his home.

Sensing that he'd spent too much time in the open, Paul clenched his fingers together just hard enough to feel the man's neck cave in between them. He felt, more than heard, the crunch of the man's windpipe being smashed together and when he dropped the shotgunner, Paul felt as though he was letting go of a heavy rag doll rather than a man. The body dropped to the floor with arms and legs sprawled in every direction. The shotgun fell against his feet.

The sickening knowledge of what he'd just done filled Paul's stomach with cold bile. Pushing it aside as best as he could, he reached down and picked up the discarded shotgun as another pair of shots went off behind him. Paul spun around to find Shay and Ellis looking up at him with blatant fear in their eyes.

The old man was glancing between Clint and Paul, unable

to make his mouth form the words he wanted to say. Shay got her hand up and pointed toward the other end of the room.

When Paul looked to where she was indicating, he was just in time to see the leader of the gunmen drop to the floor with a fresh, bloody hole in his chest.

The first thing Clint saw was the shotgun turning around toward him. His instinct was to fire high and to the side so he could catch the man behind the gun in the head or chest. But then he caught a glimpse of who that man was and managed to hold back before his finger pulled the trigger back all the way.

Paul's face reflected not the slightest bit of relief at avoiding that bullet. In fact, he had the cold look about him of someone who might just start shooting anyway.

But Clint wasn't as concerned about that as he was about what he saw behind Paul and all the others. The front door to the house had swung open during the gunfight and was now rattling against the side of the building. Through it, Clint could make out at least five other men heading toward the house. Some had torches in their hands, but all of them were carrying guns.

Paul felt his senses starting to return after he caught sight of his wife's body against the wall. Unable to muster enough strength to move his muscles, his arms hung down to his sides and he dropped to his knees as his head drooped forward. He didn't even have enough strength to cry as his world began to spin perilously around him.

"Clint, are you all right?"

Looking from the door toward the source of the voice, Clint saw Shay walking toward him. When he saw her stepping between himself and the open door, Clint dove to the side with his arms outstretched, driving his shoulder into Shay's torso and pitching them both to the floor.

Shay had seen the first signs of Clint's movement, but wasn't fast enough to do anything besides brace herself for the impact. Dull pain flooded through her body as she was taken off her feet. Her landing wasn't as bad as she thought it would be, but it still managed to knock the wind from her lungs.

At first, she thought the rumble she heard was just her insides getting rattled inside of her. But then she heard more of them. The sounds got closer and soon she recognized them as more gunshots coming from outside.

Clint acted out of pure instinct. He'd seen the approaching figures outside and spotted the guns in their hands. The first thing he'd imagined was the entire house getting shot from every direction, killing everyone inside. But then he'd seen them lining up and getting ready to file inside.

The next thing he knew, he was flying through the air and roughly sending Shay to the floor just as the men outside opened fire on the house.

"Paul, get down!" Clint yelled over the echoing blasts.

Paul was already on his knees and he began crawling toward Sarah's lifeless body.

Clint looked around for Ellis and found the old man huddled in the doorway leading to the bedroom. He had both hands over his head and was rocking back and forth.

The calamity had come, all right. And it looked to be shaping up into a full-scale slaughter.

THIRTY-TWO

It had taken Tannen less than an hour to pull together enough men for him to feel comfortable about taking on Clint Adams head on. Barstow had kept Split Creek stocked with his men, just like in Modillo. Both towns were home to a small garrison that spent most of their time patrolling the streets like an amateur army. Although both towns were a far cry from being fortified against attack, they were well protected enough to make the ones in charge stretch out and get comfortable in their roles as would-be generals.

Tannen often thought of his men as the elite of Barstow's fighters. And when he'd gathered Split Creek's reserves and headed toward the little house near the edge of town, he felt like he was leading a charge.

It had all started when a local ran into a few of Tannen's men outside of the town's little white church. Tannen had been standing to one side, keeping an eye out for familiar faces when he saw the local get cornered. There was an exchange of words and a few shouted threats, which all ended once the local turned and led the gunmen back down the street.

"We found them" was all Tannen needed to hear to figure out what the scuffle had been about.

Now, less than an hour later, Tannen stood outside and listened to the sound of gunshots coming from inside the house he'd surrounded. He stood in front of the building with the bulk of the local troops along with three of the men who were always at his side. Some of the other townspeople saw the gunmen circling around the house, but they knew better than to interfere.

Tannen heard the shooting fade away once a couple more shots went off.

One of his most loyal men stood to Tannen's right. That one shifted his feet anxiously and stared at the house. "Should we check inside?" he asked.

Tannen stared at the building for a bit and nodded. "Yeah, but take it slow. If there's anyone left in there, we don't want them to know how many of us there are."

"Right." Tannen's soldier signaled for some of the others and they all made their way toward the house.

Staying behind, Tannen removed his gun from its holster and ran his tongue over his gritty yellowed teeth. It was about damn time Barstow got off his ass and took the offensive. Looking from his gun to the house, Tannen cocked back the hammer and watched as the door swung open on its hinges.

"I'll be damned," Tannen said when he spotted Clint Adams staring straight back at him. As loud as he could, Tannen screamed, "Kill them!"

As ordered, the lead started to fly and the smoke started to pour out from the gun barrels and roll toward the house.

The charge had been sounded.

For the people inside the house, everything had just been blown inside out. Shay could hear panicked screams mixed in with the pounding roar of gunfire and could still feel the dried blood on her hands. The blood had come from her friend Sarah's body, which now lay like a discarded pile of rags on the floor. The screaming, she suddenly realized, was her own.

Ellis had been trying to stay out of the way ever since the first three men had barged through the door. By now, his entire body was in pain and he could barely get a thought to run a straight line through his head. He'd seen violence and death in his life, but had never been so close to it as he was right now. Somehow, he managed to crawl away from the bedroom door and reach out to grab hold of the .45 dropped by one of the dead killers. His hands shook uncontrollably and at any second, he fully expected to feel the burning touch of lead entering his body.

Huddled down over Sarah, Paul reached out to stroke her hair back away from her eyes one last time before opening the shotgun and plucking out its spent cartridges. He didn't think about defending the others or even taking revenge on his wife's murderers. All he thought about was getting those sons of bitches away from his house. The house was his and Sarah's home and nobody was going to take that away from him. Paul grabbed hold of the dead shotgunner's foot and pulled him closer so he could feel inside the man's pockets. Sure enough, there were a few more shells tucked away inside his jacket. Paul jammed two fresh shells into the shotgun and snapped it closed.

Clint looked around to all the others as the bullets flew around his head. As far as he could tell, Sarah was the only one hurt so far. Shay squirmed beneath him, but she seemed to be scared more than anything else. With the ringing in his ears from all the shots going off, he could barely even tell she was screaming until he leaned in close to say something to her.

"Shay," he said urgently into her ear. "Shay, you've got to quiet down and listen to me."

It took her a few seconds, but she eventually saw that Clint was saying something and managed to fight the cries back down to the back of her throat. "Sarah's dead, Clint. She's dead." Holding up her hands, Shay felt tears burning at the corners of her eyes.

"I know, but we have to get moving or else we're all going to die in this house. Do you understand me?"

She nodded weakly at first, but then she choked back her sobbing and got a hold of herself. An intense calm fell over her face like a shadow and she lowered her hands so she couldn't see the blood as she wiped it onto her dress. "I'm ready," she said. "Just please let's get out of here."

"I'm working on it." Clint looked around and chanced a peek toward the front door. The shooting had tapered off to just a few stray rounds pumped in by the occasional over-anxious trigger finger. He then looked over to Paul, who was turning and starting to walk for the door. "What the hell are you doing?" Clint said before the other man stepped into the firing line.

Paul turned to look over his shoulder. He held the shotgun ready in his hands. "I'm not letting them have this place."

Clint kept low and dashed across the room to grab Paul by the back of his shirt. The redheaded man took a fierce swing at him with the stock of the shotgun, but Clint's reflexes were prepared for just about anything and he easily dodged the blow. With one mighty shove, Clint got Paul away from the door just as another barrage of lead chewed up the entryway.

"You wanna die?" Clint shouted over the gunfire. "Then pick a better moment. If you help us, we can all get out of here."

"But my Sarah—"

"Is gone," Clint finished bluntly. "Don't you think she'd want you to live? Don't you think she'd want you to at least fight these bastards before they kill anyone else? Do you really think she'd want you to commit suicide like you were just about to do?"

Clint's words seemed to affect Paul more than any of the explosions coming from outside, the bullets tearing through the walls, or even the approaching footsteps thumping onto his front porch. He considered them for less than a second before bowing his head and nodding.

"I know what she'd want," Paul said as his face shifted back to normal. "She'd want me to drive these sons of bitches out of our town."

Clint replaced the spent cartridges in his Colt with fresh ones and snapped back the hammer. "Then let's do it."

THIRTY-THREE

Tannen stood back and watched his men creep up toward the house as if he was a spectator at an arena fight. He'd heard something about how folks in ancient times used to watch men fight to the death. At the moment, Tannen felt like he could relate to just about everyone in those stories. He was a spectator and would soon be a combatant.

Yes, indeed, this promised to be one hell of a night.

The first man to step up close to the door could hear the sounds of a woman crying. Although he couldn't see much of anything inside the house besides a lot of smoke and over-turned furniture, he hadn't really been expecting to find much else after all the lead they'd put through that place. He took another tentative step and then caught sight of a pair of boots laying on the floor.

Inching forward, he saw the boots were still wrapped around a pair of feet that were sprawled out amid some more debris. Whoever was wearing them must be flat on their back. This brought a smile to his face and brought him just a little closer so he could get a look at who this dead man was. If it was Clint Adams, then their job was already done.

The woman kept on crying as the man up front signaled for some of the others to come up closer. "Cover me," he whispered over his shoulder. "I'm going in."

He stepped inside and caught a glimpse of the corpse's

lower body and then its torso. Some of the other boys were climbing the stairs behind him, which gave the man an extra surge of confidence. The surge was just enough for him to poke his head inside and get a good look at who was left within the house.

The first thing he noticed was the grin on the dead man's face. Then he saw the shotgun in his hands.

"Adios, asshole," Paul growled as he emptied one of the shotgun's barrels into the first man's chest.

The explosion of lead tore a hole through the intruder's chest big enough to see through and the impact lifted him clean off his feet. His body sailed backward and crashed into one of the others following behind him, sending them both sprawling to the porch.

There were two others right outside the door who remained on their feet. When they saw their partner get blown into bloody chunks in front of them, they had to fight back the impulse to simply turn tail and run.

Tannen heard the shotgun and saw one of his local soldiers come sailing through the doorway. He knew right then that the tide had turned, just as he knew that he needed to make sure none of his men lost their nerve. "You two," he barked, pointing at the pair standing on the porch. "Get in there and finish them off! Shoot through the damn windows if they're watching the door!"

The two men looked back at Tannen and nodded their heads. One of them crouched down low and went for the door anyway, but the other ran around to the closest window.

"Did you hear that?" Shay asked as she helped Ellis reload the pistol he'd found.

Clint nodded and helped Paul get back to his feet. All the while, he kept his gun hand free and his eye on the door for when the next intruder decided to try his luck.

As soon as Paul was standing up, he cocked the second hammer on the shotgun and prepared himself to fire again. Until this day, he'd never fired at anything bigger than a rabbit. Until this day, he'd never thought he could kill a man. But that changed in the blink of an eye. He was ready to kill again, right now. In fact, he was anxious for it.

Pressing his back against the wall next to the door, Clint listened for even the slightest sound to drift in from outside. He figured they wouldn't open fire on the entire house just yet since their men were moving in so close, but that was hardly any reason to celebrate.

Shay was still crying, but she'd managed to keep just enough of her wits about her to function. Although her sobbing was part of the plan to cover the sound of the others moving about the place when the most recent group of killers had walked up to the door, those tears were hard to stop once they'd started and they made her voice sound shaky and fragile. "I think they're coming toward—"

Clint silenced her with a quick wave. He was still inching toward the door, his hand drifting toward an overturned chair laying on the floor.

The intruder crept forward on the porch, confident that if he got inside quickly, he could mop up some of the survivors while there was still time to get another kill under his belt. He heard the voice that was crying say something and then it was silenced again. The smell of the shotgun still hung heavy in the air, but that only served to put the man on his guard even more as he stepped forward and raised his gun to cover his entry.

Initially, all the man saw was a blur of movement coming in his direction from the inside of the house. The thing in motion wasn't as big as a man, and it was shaped like three or four sticks all pieced together. He moved to take a shot at it or anyone following behind it, but he wasn't fast enough to avoid getting hit by the incoming chair, which caught the intruder right in the face. One set of wooden posts made contact with his chin while the other set caved in his nose and drove the bones from his skull up into his brain. The guy was dead before his back hit the ground.

Paul watched Shay's face from the other side of the window as she looked outside for him. As soon as her eyes grew wide and frightened, he stood up to his full height and swung

the end of the shotgun out and around until it went straight
through the glass and pounded against flesh.

The momentum of his blow brought Paul around and in
front of the window just in time to see the man on the other
side of it reeling back in pain. Beneath the shattering glass
and shuffling steps, there was the sound of a sharp intake of
breath and the distinct grunt of pain. Paul smiled at those
sounds and waited for the wounded man to raise his head up
again before pulling the shotgun's trigger.

Belching out a wave of thunder and slamming against
Paul's shoulder, the shotgun erupted with a spray of hot lead
and black smoke, turning the intruder's head into a pulpy
crimson mist.

"Ok," Clint said after pitching the chair to the ground.
"Those were our free shots. Now, things are going to get
tricky."

THIRTY-FOUR

Sheriff Furlan had gotten word about the men gathering near Paul and Sarah's house, but really didn't know quite what to make of it. As far as he knew, Paul had kept his nose clean and not even Barstow would have any reason to start any nasty business with him. So when he heard about the gathering, he didn't really think too much of it.

Then the shooting had started.

Furlan knew that Barstow didn't need any particular reason to focus his attention on anybody, but it was usually just a matter of him looking for some kind of favor or handout. After all, that was how this part of the country worked. The lawman tried to keep that in mind as he rushed through town on his way to Paul's house. He hoped against hope that he wouldn't find a mess that was too far out of control.

What he found, in fact, was much worse than he could have ever thought possible.

The place looked like a small battlefield. He'd heard the crackle of gunfire on his way over, but when he rounded the corner and got within sight of the little house, a shotgun blast echoed through the air like an approaching storm. It was at that moment that Furlan realized he'd heard that noise earlier and had chosen to ignore it. At the time, he'd thought it was some of Barstow's men letting off steam, or even a fight at one of the saloons.

Now, he saw where it had come from and the bottom of

his stomach fell completely away. If anything happened to that poor couple of kids while he'd just stood by and watched . . .

"What in God's name is going on here?" Furlan bellowed as he ran up to the first man he could reach.

The sheriff didn't recognize who he was talking to besides the simple fact that he was one of the gunmen owned by Matt Barstow. When the gunman shrugged and turned around as though he was looking at a child throwing a tantrum, Furlan nearly took a swing at the guy out of sheer principle.

"I'm talking to you, boy," Furlan seethed.

Hearing that, the gunman spun around and his hand flashed toward his pistol. Although he still didn't talk to the lawman, he began storming toward him.

Suddenly, a hand latched onto the gunman's shoulder and pulled him away from the sheriff. "Don't mind him," Tannen said once he had the gunman's attention. "You take orders from me. Now get back to work before I take a shot at you myself."

There was another eruption of gunfire coming from the house, but Tannen didn't even flinch. "I'd appreciate it if you let my men do their work, Sheriff."

"Since when does Barstow send in an army to shoot up an innocent couple's home?" Furlan said with rage burning at the edge of his voice. "I'm still the law here and I cannot allow this!"

The gunman that Furlan had first approached looked between Tannen and the sheriff as though he wasn't sure which way to jump. "Those folks inside are puttin' up more of a fight than we thought," he said to Tannen, while keeping a leery eye on Furlan. "Should we all charge in there?"

Without looking away from the sheriff, Tannen said, "Yes. Do it quickly before they get too dug in or have enough time to think about what they should do."

Furlan shook his head and gripped his gun. "I don't give a shit about what Barstow's trying to do here. You're not going in there shooting. For all we know, your men have already shot down that couple."

Tannen sent his soldier into the battle with a backhanded slap across his chest. The gunman turned and stalked toward the house, breaking into a run as another crackle of gunfire came from the building.

"What you gonna do about that?" Tannen asked as he stepped up to the sheriff with his chest puffed out like a strutting rooster.

Looking from Tannen to the home of Paul and Sarah, Furlan considered just how far he wanted to push Barstow's representative. He knew the powerful land owner could just as easily make his house the target of the next attack. But then again, Furlan also thought about the time he'd spent inside the house that was being shot at right now. Furlan had had supper in there as Paul's guest. He'd tasted Sarah's cooking. Now, he could hear the echoes of what he thought were her screams ringing in his ears.

"This is what I'm gonna do about it," Furlan said as he drew his pistol and brought it up.

Before the gun was even readied to fire, the sheriff was stopped by another crack of gunfire. This time, it didn't come from the house, but from the weapon in Tannen's hand.

Furlan blinked a few times as a painful heat surged through his body that was followed by a warm wetness running down his front. When he lifted his hand to see what it was, it came back covered in a layer of blood so thick it almost looked black. The sheriff tried to talk, but couldn't draw in enough air to form the words. All he could do was gasp once and drop to his knees.

As soon as Furlan hit the ground, Tannen sent a boot up into the wounded man's chin. The sound of teeth slamming together was almost as jarring as the explosions in the distance. "You picked the wrong time to grow a conscience, Sheriff," Tannen said with a filthy smile. "But thanks for stopping by. I'll send the folks inside your best wishes."

When he turned toward the house, Tannen saw that most of his men were looking at the sheriff's body with a look of stunned surprise on their faces. He ignored their gaping stares and headed for the front porch. There was a group of five of his soldiers huddled on either side of the door, holding their guns out, but not making an attempt to step inside.

"What's taking you?" Tannen growled. "I thought I said for you to charge inside and finish this off."

The man farthest from the door nodded quickly. "I know you did, sir, but every time we get close—"

Suddenly a volley of gunfire erupted from within the house, followed by a blast from a shotgun. Although most of what sounded like pistol shots whipped through the front door and through the shattered frame, the shotgun seemed to be directed elsewhere. Before Tannen could wonder where it was being shot, he heard an agonized scream and the thump of a body hitting the dirt.

Tannen looked around the corner to see one of the soldiers he'd sent to circle around the place rolling on the ground, clutching at the bloody stump that used to be his arm.

"Every time we get close," the man on the porch continued, "they pull something like that."

With his blood already boiling from talking to the sheriff, Tannen cocked back the hammer of his pistol and shoved the weapon into the closest man's face. "You get your asses up those stairs or I'll put you all down," he seethed. "Now on my mark, I want all of you to move inside and keep shooting until there ain't nothing left to shoot at."

Tannen looked around the side of the house to make sure all of his men had heard what he'd said. Once he saw them all get ready to move, Tannen steeled himself. "One . . .

THIRTY-FIVE

The inside of the little house had almost completely filled up with smoke. The fog rolled in from the barrels of all the guns that had gone off inside the place, giving it the smell of a battlefield rather than somebody's home. Clint and Ellis sent bullets through the front door whenever there were more men about to come inside. Paul had just used up another shotgun round and Clint turned to see what was going on in the other room.

"I hope you didn't waste that ammunition," Clint said over his shoulder.

Paul's voice sounded unnaturally cool and collected. "I'd say it served its purpose well enough."

Shay sat huddled in one corner with a pistol clutched in her hands, trying not to panic amid all the chaos. "Are we about ready to get out of here?" she asked.

Clint sidled up to one of the windows and peeked over the sill. He'd been organizing the others to stay in relatively safe spots where they could fire and not be in too much danger, but those spots were being chipped away awful quickly. His mind raced for ways to turn this situation around. He'd already seen one innocent person get killed and he wasn't about to let another one die in front of his eyes. On the other hand, with the cards going against him this badly, Clint didn't have any safe options to choose from.

Looking out through what was left of the window, Clint

147

noticed that the men outside had pulled away for the moment, but were clustering up into a few distinct groups. "Looks like they're pulling away," he said.

"That's good," Ellis grunted as he dug through a dead man's pockets looking for more bullets.

Shaking his head, Clint said, "Well, the bad news is that they look like they're getting ready to move in all at once."

"Oh," Ellis said. "That's bad."

"Yeah. It is."

Until this moment, Paul had been standing where he'd been told and shooting at what he saw. But now, he wheeled around to face Clint, making sure not to look down at the body of his wife. "You said you could figure a way out of this."

"I can, but I don't want to be responsible for getting anyone else hurt."

"You're not the one who did this," Paul said as he hung his head down low. "This is all my fault. I brought them here."

Clint looked at the redhead and thought back to when the first set of gunmen had walked into the house. It seemed so long ago and Paul's sorrowful apology still hung heavily in the air. "From everything I've seen and heard around here, I doubt you had much choice in the matter. Besides, we got to worry about staying alive right now. If we're going to try something, we've got to do it quick, before they all storm in at once."

"Well, what did you have in mind?" Paul asked.

Clint looked around the small home for about the hundredth time since the shooting had started. There wasn't a lot to work with. Besides the old cast-iron stove and the kitchen table, the main room was filled with nothing else besides clutter and the occasional body. "What else is in the bedroom?"

Ellis spoke up before anyone else. "There's a bigger bed and a dresser. Not much else besides that."

Just then, something dawned on Clint that had been nagging from the back of his mind all this time. He looked at the walls, which had been shot up so badly that light streamed in from all kinds of odd angles as men walked by and blocked first one and then another. Although there were plenty of them, the holes seemed to be higher up than they needed to be.

He expected that not all of the shots would come in from the same place, but more often than not, the bullets seemed to be passing high enough over their heads for them to duck beneath them. While Clint's first instinct had told him to get out as soon as possible, there was something else that told him that he did have some time. Now, looking at the odd placement of those bullet holes, he knew where that second part had come from.

Shay came up close to him, clutching a pistol so tight that her knuckles had turned white. "What are we gonna do, Clint?"

"We're going to call their bluff."

Every face in the house turned toward him, each one wearing a similar shocked expression.

"What bluff?" Paul asked. "They seem pretty serious to me."

"He's right," Ellis said. "They killed Sarah. How much more serious do you want them to get?"

Clint took another look out the window and saw the groups of gunmen readying themselves for another onslaught. He then ran to the bedroom and took a look outside of the window there. Sure enough, that side was all but clear with only two men standing casually to either side.

Running back to the main room, Clint motioned for the others to follow him, saying, "They're herding us toward the back."

Although Shay was more than happy to get away from the front door, she didn't seem too excited about what Clint was saying, either. "What do you mean? We can't get out that way! There's no door!"

"No, but there's a window and only two men watching it," Clint said as he pushed Shay into the bedroom. "They're leaving us an opening and right now we don't have much choice but to take it."

Ellis shrugged and followed Shay, but Paul wasn't so prepared to leave. "What happens once we get out there?" he asked.

Clint could feel the attack drawing closer and could even hear Tannen's voice barking commands from the front porch. "I honestly don't know," he said. "But whatever it is, at least it'll be out there where we have a chance. If they wanted us dead, they could have stampeded in here or even set fire to the place."

"Maybe they really don't think we'll try to go through that window," Paul said.

"If that's the case, then I'll be real happy to admit I was wrong. But either way, we need to be out of here when they decide to make their play."

Just then, Tannen's voice became a bellowing growl as he screamed at his men and told them to get ready to move.

"On my mark . . ." he shouted.

"Time's up," Clint said as he turned to head for the smaller room. "Do whatever you want."

Paul took one more look at his wife and leaned down to quickly touch her cheek. Then he ran for the bedroom to help Clint and Ellis lift the small dresser. Between all three of the men, they got the piece of furniture up on their shoulders.

"As soon as this goes through," Clint said, "we're up and out the window. Keep running and we'll meet up at the livery."

"One . . ." Tannen shouted from outside as Clint and the others steadied their grips on the dresser.

"Two . . ."

As one, all three men swung the dresser back before moving it forward like an awkward battering ram.

"Three!"

The dresser left their hands and crashed through the glass just as footsteps began pounding over the front porch and gunshots once again riddled the little house.

THIRTY-SIX

When all the commotion started up again, the noises blended together to form a single whirlwind of sound that wrapped around the house like a giant fist. Its tendrils reached through the door and stabbed out through the windows to spike into the eardrums of every soul that was close enough to hear.

First came the crash of broken glass and the dresser hitting the ground. Shay was already standing on the headboard and jumping out by the time stampeding footsteps sounded from the other room. Tiny shards of broken glass sliced into her palms and feet as she cleared the window frame, but there wasn't enough to do any serious damage.

Next, Ellis all but threw himself out the window and landed on one of the gunmen waiting outside. Of the two that had been positioned next to the rear window, only one was left standing. The other had been knocked over by the piece of flying furniture.

"Go on," Clint said as he shoved Paul toward the newly created opening. "I'll be right behind you."

Paul didn't take too much time to think as he jumped on top of the bed and sprung headfirst out the window. Holding the shotgun in front of him, he managed to clear the frame with only a few cuts to show for it. The landing was helped as well, since the shotgun was the first thing to hit the ground. Paul tucked his body in and managed to perform a sloppy roll before scrambling to his feet.

Clint stood with his back to the window, waiting for the gunmen to start charging inside the house. The first ones through the door were looking wildly about and seemed confused by the fact that there was nobody on their feet to greet them. Although Clint couldn't see everything through the bedroom door, he could see enough to know when he was spotted.

As soon as he heard Paul land outside, Clint saw the gunmen in the front room look toward the door. They spotted him almost immediately and raised their guns to fire. Clint's hand flashed upward and sent two rounds through the air. Both of his bullets struck home and took the two men off their feet before they could squeeze their triggers. Before those two hit the floor, Clint reached out and slammed the door shut.

"Come on!" Shay shouted from outside.

Just as Clint wondered about the two gunmen that had been beyond the window, he heard a thundering roar from Paul's shotgun. Clint started to bolt for the window, but then he heard more voices filling the other room. Knowing they would be making their way into the bedroom at any second, he quickly holstered his gun and grabbed hold of the bottom of the bed frame with both hands. Clint's muscles, fueled by the adrenaline in his veins and the thumping of his heart, strained within his body, allowing him to lift the end of the bed and shove the entire frame against the door with one straining motion.

As soon as the wooden legs slammed down, the door was kicked in by the men on the other side, opening less than an inch before crashing against the bed. The door rattled violently on its hinges as more and more hands shoved against it. When no shots were fired through the barricade, Clint felt even more confident in his theory that Tannen wanted them to take the path they'd chosen.

He decided to worry about that later, however, as he turned and took a running leap for the window. Clint's body sailed through the air and easily went through the shattered pane. One jagged piece of glass raked along his stomach, but Clint barely even noticed. Even the impact of his body against the fallen dresser did little more than rattle his bones as he rolled off and came up with gun in hand.

One of the gunmen was on his side with his arms laying askew to one side. The other was flat on his back, his chest and stomach spread wide open and blackened by close-range gunfire.

"Is everyone all right?" Clint asked.

There were nods all around, even though they were all bleeding from their exit through the shattered window.

More gunshots came from the house, followed by shouting voices. Tannen's could be heard among them, but it was just a thread inside a wild and chaotic tapestry of sound. Besides, Clint didn't have to hear the words in order to have a good idea of what they were.

"Start running for the stables," he said. "If you see them coming after you, try to lose them and circle back around."

Every one of them were moving as fast as their feet could carry them. Ellis and Shay had gotten a head start, but were only about ten feet in front of Paul and Clint. Although the sounds of battle were nipping at their heels, those were the only things that followed them as they raced through the alleys and headed for the stable.

By the sound of it, Tannen's men were about to bring the walls of the house down around their ears if they kept going at their current rate. Despite the rushed orders he'd given, a few of them had started shooting at the door when they saw that it wasn't about to budge on its own.

"Hold it," Tannen shouted after he got to the door and tried to move it himself. Turning to look at the men bringing up the rear, he stabbed a finger toward the back of the house. "I want some of you to go and check the rear of this place. The rest of you men get that door open. I don't care if you have to tear it off with your bare hands."

When he saw that his orders were being carried out, Tannen went out through the front door and ran around the building behind the men he'd sent. The first thing he saw when he came around back was the body of the first man that had been opened up by a shotgun. Next, Tannen saw the dresser sitting amid the broken glass and then he found the second gunman he'd posted to watch the back.

Of the three men that had gone to look, one of them had already taken off running toward the nearby alleys.

"Stop where you are," Tannen ordered.

Although he looked back in obvious confusion, the man who'd been running halted as he he'd been told.

Tannen motioned for all three of them to come back. "If they've managed to get that far, then they could be just waiting for us to follow them. Besides," he added as he scanned the bodies laying beneath the window, "it looks like he's still with them. If that's the case, then we already know where they're headed."

After a few seconds ticked by, Tannen raised his gun into the air and let off a few shots. "We can't let them get away too easily, though," he said. "*Now* you can go after them."

The three men took off toward the alleys like a pack of bloodthirsty hounds. By that time, Tannen could hear the sounds of wood being broken apart coming from inside the house, as well as footsteps coming up behind him. He holstered his gun and turned around to face the two that had come to check up on what he was doing.

"Go back and tell the men that our prey has already been flushed out and has flown the coop," Tannen said calmly to one of the men who rode with him on a steady basis. "Round up the rest of us and get them ready to pull out of town. Tell the locals to stay here and make sure nobody finds out about Sheriff Furlan just yet."

All three of Tannen's remaining cowboys had gathered outside the house. The rest were thugs drawn from the local pool.

"Where's Kel?" Tannen asked as he turned and started walking toward the nearest street.

"He caught one before we charged inside," one of the cowboys answered. "What about you? Where are you headed?"

"I'll send a message to Barstow. He'll want to know what happened here."

"How pissed do you think he'll be?"

Tannen was out near the front of the house when he looked

back with his familiar dirty smile on his face. The darkly stained teeth inside his mouth almost glistened in what little light there was. "Pissed? He'd only be pissed if things didn't go exactly the way he'd wanted them to go. The way I see it, this night couldn't have gone any better."

Wheeling around to stride toward the little street that curved behind the rest of the town, Tannen could hear the sounds of wood being broken and the contents of that damn house being thrown to the ground. It seemed like the local gunmen were going to do their best to make sure nothing was left of that place when they left.

Good, Tannen thought. This would be just another thing to show the town just who was in charge and what happened to anyone who got in their way.

By the time Tannen reached the telegraph office, he felt bold enough to finish off Clint Adams all by himself.

THIRTY-SEVEN

Clint and the others made it to the livery without having to stray too far from the alleyways. They ran without stopping once and by the time they met up inside the stable, every one of them were sucking in their breaths as though their lungs were about to burst at the seams.

"Is that you, Mister Garrison?" the stable boy asked as he rushed in to see who'd just charged in through the front door.

Paul was in the middle of saddling up a black dun and didn't even take the time to look away from his task. "It sure is, Ben. You'd best get on out of here and head home. There's some men that'll be coming this way any minute."

"They comin' after you and Mister Adams?"

"That's right."

"Then I can stay behind and point them in the wrong direction after you leave. That should give you some time to—"

"No!" Paul barked as he turned to face the young boy. "Just do as I told you and get out of here. I won't have you getting hurt because of me, too."

By this time, Clint had Eclipse saddled up and ready to go. He jumped onto the Darley Arabian and helped Shay up behind him. "We don't have time for this," he said. "Take Ellis with you and follow me out." Not waiting for confirmation, Clint touched his heels to Eclipse's side and took off through the large front doors.

Paul cinched the buckle of his saddle a little tighter and

climbed into the stirrups. Ellis was right behind him. "Ben, just do as I said and get yourself . . ." Paul stopped in mid-sentence when he realized that there was nobody else in the stables besides the other horses. He looked around quickly, but couldn't catch so much as a glimpse of the boy.

Following the sounds of the Darley Arabian's steps, Paul flicked his reins and got his ride moving out of the stable and into the waiting night.

THIRTY-EIGHT

Clint rode toward the edge of Split Creek, heading for the trail that would lead him back in the direction of Modillo. Before he made it to the open range, however, he caught sight of a pair of riders who had taken up position near a small building on the outskirts of town.

He motioned for the horse behind him to veer off before breaking into the open and then turned Eclipse to head that same direction as well. Keeping to the darkened perimeter of the town, Clint easily got ahead of Paul's horse and led it toward a trail that headed southeast.

That one was left unguarded and, although he didn't like the idea of being herded even farther, Clint took that route just so they could give themselves some room to catch their breath. Once Split Creek was nothing more than a bright spot in the road behind them, Clint brought Eclipse to a stop and waited for Paul to pull up alongside of him.

It took a few moments for them all to collect themselves. In that time, all four of them sat in their saddles, breathing heavily, trying not to think too much about what they'd just been through. Finally, someone broke the tense silence that had descended over them.

"So where do we go now?" Shay asked.

Ellis swung down from behind Paul and put his hands on his hips while bending deeply at the knees. "Did I hear cor-

rectly back there about us being herded toward the back of
the house?"

"That's what I said," Clint replied.

"Then we were supposed to escape?"

Clint could feel Shay trembling behind him. Her arms
were locked around his torso and her body was pressed solidly against his back. It was as though every muscle inside
of her decided to try and shake free of their bones.

"What are you talking about?" she asked. "Why would
they have killed Sarah if they wanted us to get away?"

"Because Sarah wasn't important to them," Paul answered
in a voice that was devoid of all emotion. "All they cared
about was Adams. The rest of us didn't mean shit to them."

Clint had been watching Paul ever since they'd left town.
Even after taking the lead on the way out, he'd been sure to
keep track of the sound of Paul's horse, making certain that
it never got too far away. All the while, he'd been thinking
about what he should do with the man. Now was as good a
time as any to find out.

"Is there something you want to tell us?" Clint asked.

Shay looked back and forth between Clint and Paul, study-
ing the way each man regarded the other. While Clint's eyes
were fixed intently on their target, Paul's were turned solemnly away . . . almost as if he was ashamed. Turning back
toward Clint, Shay asked, "What's this about?"

"That's just what I was going to ask him," Clint said.
"Why don't we start with why you apologized to me when
those first three came walking into your house."

The very mention of that incident brought a sullen shadow
over Paul's face. His eyes glazed over as though he was
reliving the moment in his mind. His fists closed tightly
around the reins.

Clint saw all of this and pressed on anyway. "You turned
me in, didn't you? You turned us all in to Barstow's men."

"I didn't have a choice," Paul said in a voice that was like
steam being forced through a cold metal piston. "Tannen
knew someone had taken you in and was telling everyone
that whoever got caught with you would be burned out of

their home. I've seen him pull things like that, Mister Adams."

"Did you ever see him pull something like what happened back there?"

Again, Paul's eyes glazed over. When he snapped back into the present, his expression was cut from stone and his mouth was a single chiseled line. "No. Never."

Shay dropped down from the saddle and went over to Paul's side. Once there, she reached up and put a hand on his knee and pat him soothingly. Turning to Clint, she said, "You don't understand. He didn't have a choice. If you live in these parts, you either do what Barstow's men say or you pay the price. Please don't be too hard on him."

"There's nothing I can do," Clint said, "that could be any worse than what has already happened."

Paul looked up from the point at which he'd been staring and locked his gaze onto Clint. Pain was written all over his face. It etched lines into his skin that would probably be there for the rest of his days.

Stepping forward, Clint put a hand on his shoulder. "I can see what Barstow and Tannen have been putting you and all of these people through. I know you didn't have any choice. All I want to know is what they told you."

"Tannen wanted to know who was hiding you all and where you were," Paul explained. "He and some of his men were standing out by the church because they knew most of the town would show up for the social. Sarah was . . ." His voice stuck in the back of his throat and a tear dripped from the corner of his eye. After coughing and rubbing away the trickle of water with the back of his hand, Paul was able to go on. "Sarah was afraid that they'd start roughing folks up until they found out what they wanted."

"They've done that plenty of times before," Ellis added.

"Well, my Sarah didn't want no one to get hurt because of what we done, so she asked me what she should do. Tannen must've heard because he came over to us and started . . . pushing us both around."

It was obvious that thinking about what had happened was starting another fire deep inside of Paul's guts. "I tried to fight them, but I couldn't. Dammit to hell," he said while slamming a fist into the palm of his other hand. "I just couldn't do anything to make them leave us alone."

Clint let the other man stew for a bit until he thought Paul was ready to talk again. "What did they say once you told them where we were?"

Taking a deep breath, Paul didn't even try to look Clint in the eyes when he answered. "They wanted us to get the first three inside before you had a chance to get ready for them. Tannen said if we did good enough, that he'd let me and Sarah get away before the shooting started."

"Was there anything else? Anything at all?"

Paul thought for a few seconds and shook his head. Then suddenly his eyes lit up and he looked as though he'd had a revelation. "Yes! He said something about running you out of town. Running you all the way to Ander's Valley."

"Where's Ander's Valley?"

"It's the next town over," Shay replied. "About a day or so's ride east of here."

Clint turned and walked slowly back to Eclipse. Even after all the time they'd taken to stop and talk things over, he still couldn't hear the sound of anyone on their tail. "If Tannen was herding us in a certain direction, then maybe he was trying to get us to run for Ander's Valley. Is there any reason for him or Barstow to want that?"

Silence dropped over the group like an unwelcome rain. After a few seconds that dragged by like a horse with two clubbed feet, it was finally broken by Ellis's gruff, harsh voice.

"Hell," the old man said. "Maybe if he puts on a big enough show in Ander's Valley, than Barstow would finally be able to get his hooks into the place."

"What?" Clint said as he turned around.

Ellis took a step back as though he'd been scolded. "I don't think Barstow has much to do with Ander's Valley. Not yet, anyway."

"I'll be damned," Clint said after thinking over what Ellis had just told them.

"Am I missing something?" Shay asked, a look of confusion twisting her mouth down at the corners.

"Barstow rules his towns by force," Clint pointed out excitedly. "Or at least through threats of force. He got Modillo by shooting down the sheriff." Turning to Paul, he asked, "And how did he get into Split Creek?"

"We had some desperadoes come through town and Tannen's boys put them underground. After that, they stayed on and nobody was brave enough to take them on."

Snapping his fingers, Clint beamed with the revelation. "And if Barstow's men take down somebody famous enough, they just might get to expand into another town."

"But Ander's Valley is a big place," Ellis pointed out. "That's a railroad town."

"Which is why Barstow needs a bigger spectacle to get his foot in the door."

Suddenly, Shay's face dropped and she rushed back over to Clint's side. "How big a spectacle are you talking about?"

"The bigger the better."

Ellis whistled softly and shook his head slowly. "Well, they don't get much bigger than the death of the Gunsmith. That'd be big enough to make the whole damn town be scared of Barstow's boys."

"Oh, Clint," Shay said as she wrapped her arms around him. By the way she held on, it seemed as though she figured on holding him in that spot for the rest of their lives. "Please tell me you're not going to go."

Gently pulling away from her, Clint swung back up onto Eclipse's back. "I don't see any other way for this to end. Barstow won't just back down if he loses me and I can't turn my back on what's going on. Besides," he added with a wink, "if it's a spectacle Barstow wants . . . maybe that's just what he deserves."

THIRTY-NINE

Convinced that there wouldn't be anyone preventing him from getting to Ander's Valley, Clint decided to give the overworked horses a rest and take the trail at a leisurely pace. Eclipse was far from exhausted, but the nag carrying Paul and Ellis looked less than appreciative for the extra burden.

As night fully enveloped them, Clint lifted his eyes to the sky and took in a long, healthy dose of the stars overhead. Without so much as a campfire to take away from their majesty, the pinpoints of light winked down at them all like supportive angels that approved of the task they'd taken on.

After a while, every one of the travelers was able to calm down enough for the tension crackling around them to dissipate and eventually bleed off into the air. Even though he was the one with the target painted on his forehead, Clint was the first one to relax and immerse himself in the breathtaking nighttime canopy.

The trail had taken them into a stretch of desert that turned the dirt beneath their feet into gritty sand and the trees along the trail into cactus. As soon as the sun's last embers had died off, the air became cool on their skin. Before too much longer it became downright cold.

"I thought I'd left all this behind me," Clint griped as he rubbed his hands together and fished a coat from where it had been stored on his saddle.

He had taken to walking beside Eclipse with the reins in

163

his hands so the Darley Arabian wouldn't have to carry him and Shay both. A gout of expelled air came from the horse's nostrils in the form of a burst of steam that felt warm on Clint's shoulder.

"Left what behind?" Shay asked from atop the stallion.

Clint eased into the coat and slid on a worn pair of gloves. "The cold. I rode all the way through the Rockies and northern territories to make it this far south just to get away from the damn cold. Now here it is again. Feels like it's following me."

Shay smiled and turned her head so that her hair fell down to cover her neck. It was all the shelter she seemed to need from the chilling darkness. "I like it. Makes me feel alive and clean."

"A bath is all I need to feel clean. And make it a hot one while you're at it. As for feeling alive ... I can think of plenty of other things that don't involve freezing that make me feel just as alive." Looking up at Shay, Clint added, "Even more so."

Ahead of them, Paul walked next to his horse, leading it by the reins. He didn't walk with any spring in his step or even any response to the sudden onset of cold. Instead, he simply dropped one foot in front of the other, staring ahead to the point where the trail disappeared within the inky black. He didn't say a word besides what was required to answer the occasional question.

Just one foot in front of the other ... onward and onward as long as he could get them to move.

Behind him, Ellis sat in the saddle with both hands on the knotted leather horn. His body shifted from side to side, adjusting to the motions of the animal as his head lolled about as though it had somehow become disconnected from his neck. The old man's mouth hung open to let a steady stream of snores drift out and mix with the call of coyotes in the distance.

"You don't seem too worried," Shay said after she'd managed to look away from the jewel-encrusted sky.

Shrugging, Clint asked, "Worried about what?"

"I don't know. Maybe about the gunmen that are out to

kill you. The ones that want to make your death a show for an entire town to see. The same ones you're riding toward right now."

"Maybe I'd worry more if there weren't so many others out there just as bad and worse than them. Besides, it doesn't do anybody any good to worry about something before you can do anything about. Right now, I'm just out on a beautiful night taking a slow ride beneath the stars. Not a lot to worry about there."

Shay smiled in a way that somehow pulled Clint's eyes away from the heavens. For a few moments, she just looked at him with those deep blue eyes, sizing him up. "I don't know how you did it, but you somehow managed to get me to stop worrying as well. I thought I'd never be able to sleep tonight and now I feel like I'm about to fall off this horse."

"Actually, I'm feeling the same way. I think ol' Ellis has got the right idea. Maybe we should find a spot to make camp."

Shay nodded, but didn't seem too anxious to stop riding. Instead, she let her eyes droop slightly and turned her face upward so she could once again take in the sight spread out above her.

Since there wasn't anyplace that looked too promising anyway, Clint decided to keep watch for a suitable spot, but to keep the horses moving along until that time came. Besides, Ellis was fine right where he was and Paul hadn't seemed to be entirely with them since the trip had begun. To stay awake, Clint remained on his feet, walking beside Eclipse with one hand resting on the stallion's mane.

He used the time to let the events of the last few days filter through his mind. It had all started over a game of poker. Clint had seen plenty of cheats, but not so many that were willing to go to war over getting called out about it. In fact, the more Clint thought about it, the more the cards seemed stacked against him. Not only in that game, but in this whole damn situation.

He shook the pessimism from his head and reminded himself about why he was going through all of this. To do that, all he needed was a good look at Paul. Just seeing the despair written across his face brought the vision of Sarah's dead body back into Clint's mind.

This wasn't about a card cheat or even about Barstow's passion to see Clint dead. There were too many of both kinds of people roaming about the world for Clint to lose too much sleep over them. This was all about the folks that had to live in towns like Modillo, Split Creek and Ander's Valley after Clint was long gone.

They didn't have gunmen to fight for their causes or power to fix the decisions that made their lives easier. They didn't have much of anything.

That was why Clint fought for them.

It didn't take much, but every once in a while, he needed to remind himself of why he went through all the hell that turned his life upside down. It would have been so much easier to settle down and live off his reputation for a while. He'd had books written about him and had kept company with legends, but none of that was what truly mattered.

In Clint's mind, what mattered most was using his skills to help people like Ellis and Shay. There would always be those who he would never be able to fix. Paul was one of them. Seeing the despair etched onto the redhead's features only strengthened Clint's resolve.

FORTY

Before he knew he was doing it, Clint walked up beside Paul and kept pace with him. After a minute or so, he simply looked over and said, "It wasn't your fault."

"The hell it wasn't," Paul replied bitterly.

"They would have found out sooner or later. Even if they found out after we left, Barstow wouldn't have let it go. It was his men that pulled the trigger, Paul. Not you."

"I brought them there. I didn't even think about what would happen to you . . . none of you. I just . . ."

"You were just protecting your family. Nobody can blame you for that. The way Barstow runs things, you didn't have much choice."

Paul looked over to Clint and then back down at the ground. He lifted his arm to point to a spot farther along the trail where there was a small outcropping of boulders setting in the sand. "That'd be a good place to camp."

Looking at the spot, Clint nodded his head in agreement.

The group of rocks was an even better campsite than what it appeared to be from afar. As the horses drew closer to the boulders, the trail sloped downward to form a small alcove behind the rocks that was perfect for shielding a good-sized campfire. On the side of the rocks facing away from the trail, the ground was soft and flat. Only a part of the winds that whipped across the sands made it around the natural shelter to fan the flames and cool down everyone gathered around them.

Ellis woke up just long enough to climb down off his horse and help set up the fire before finding a comfortable spot on the ground and collapsing once again. Even in the open air, his snores reverberated loudly and echoed off the sloping wall of rock.

Sitting with his legs drawn in close and his hands clasped together, Paul watched the dancing flames until he could no longer keep his eyes open. The only indication he gave that he'd actually fallen asleep was when his head dropped forward to rest upon his knees.

Clint felt the grating sting of dust in the back of his throat and fished around in his saddlebags to find what he needed to brew a cup of coffee. Luckily, he hadn't taken everything out when he'd arrived in Split Creek, so most of his supplies were still in place. As he prepared the coffee, he noticed Shay watching him from the other side of the fire.

"Care for a cup?" he asked.

"Sure."

He fished around until he dug out a smaller, more dented version of the cup he held in his hand. "I'll have to warn you . . . I'm not much of a cook. Usually, I'm the only one who can stomach the coffee I make."

"I'm sure it'll be fine," she said with a tired smile.

It felt good to lose himself in such a mundane task. Also, the chill of the desert had begun to soak down to Clint's bones, so sitting so close to the little campfire warmed him up just enough. They didn't talk while the coffee brewed, even though they watched each other closely over the roaring flames.

Shay's eyes seemed to glitter with the reflected firelight and the warm glow played off her skin the way sunlight soaked into a cloud. The little shadows dancing over her features made her seem almost unnaturally beautiful. When Clint handed her a cup of smoking java, she smiled again, pursed her lips together and gently blew off some of the rising steam.

Clint could feel a warmth running through him that had

nothing at all to do with the fire. He noticed the way the moonlight drenched her blonde hair with a soft radiance while the fire brought out some of her sharper details. When she took a sip of the coffee, she recoiled just a little.

"That's still pretty hot," he warned.

Holding the cup in both hands, Shay closed her eyes and gently ran the tip of her tongue along the edge of her lips. She opened her mouth just a little wider and set the edge of the cup onto her full lower lip. Steam rose up from the liquid and over her face as she let the hot coffee trickle into her mouth.

Looking up with just her eyes, Shay lowered the cup. "You're right," she said softly. "That is very hot."

They sat near the campfire, talking about little things that were only important to the ones speaking about them. Both Clint and Shay were glad for the distraction and welcomed any amount of time where they could put their minds toward smaller things than running for their lives.

Even though he didn't expect any trouble until he got to Ander's Valley, Clint kept one ear attuned to the noises around him. He searched for any sign of horses or footsteps coming their way and more than once, his head snapped up at the sound of an animal's voice in the distance.

"You're still watching out for us," Shay said after he'd tensed at a faraway noise. "After what I saw, I think those men would be awful stupid to come after you. Especially after how you handled all of them."

"I didn't exactly handle all of them."

"No, but you could have." Getting up, she shuffled around the fire and sat down beside Clint. "If you'd have set your mind to it, I'll bet you could have done things differently and taken them all down."

Part of Clint's mind went through the motions of re-thinking the strategy he could have used to get rid of more of Barstow's men. On some level, he'd been thinking about it ever since he heard them surrounding that house. Then he thought about something else. "You ask me a lot of questions about what I do."

Grinning widely, she leaned against his side. "It's just that

I've never seen anything like it. Never had anyone protect me like you did."

"Don't thank me yet. We're not quite done with all of this."

"Well, I still say they'd be stupid to come after us."

Clint laughed and tossed the rest of his coffee into the fire. "Nobody ever said men like that were smart."

"Do you think they'll be coming after us?"

Reflexively, Clint looked out to the open space, which spread before them like a sandy blanket. Although there wasn't much to block his view, the darkness had become a thick, murky soup that swallowed up everything too far beyond the reach of the fire's light. "Probably not. If they want us to get to Ander's Valley, then that's where they'll make their move. But that's not to say that there's no outside chance of them jumping the gun."

He could feel Shay's body tensing next to his and could hear her take in a soft, contented breath. The tin cup made a brushing sound as it was set down onto the ground, freeing her hands up so they could slide around his body.

"I feel so safe when I'm with you," she whispered.

Over the last few days, Clint had gotten more than a little used to the feel of Shay's arms wrapped around him. Her fingers dug into him when he tried to move away, but not as hard as they scratched across his bare skin when they'd given in to what they both desired the most. He could still feel those touches on his naked back and he could still smell the musky scent of her body's natural fragrance.

As if reading his mind, Shay slipped her hand down along Clint's thigh until she could rub between his legs. She pressed her lips against his neck and brushed them up until she could gently lick his ear. "It's such a beautiful night," she said, her breath hot against his skin. "Let's not waste it."

All of the fatigue that had been wearing down Clint's system suddenly vanished as he got up and helped Shay to her feet. He knew he should keep an eye out just in case Tannen and his gunmen decided to make their play early. He also knew that it would be best to get his sleep while there was time to do so.

But then again, Clint knew a few other things as well. For instance, he knew how good it felt to have Shay's hands on him. Even through his clothing, her touch was enough to make him yearn for much, much more. Their skin touched as she took his hand, giving Clint a sample of just how soft her flesh was and how warm it could be against his own.

More than anything, he knew that he wanted her. And if moments like this were allowed to slip by, he knew he would regret it.

FORTY-ONE

Shay led him to a spot behind the rocks and out of the wavering firelight. When they moved into the shadows, they could feel a chill creep over their skin, which was instantly chased away as they turned and embraced while kissing each other deeply on the mouth.

Clint's hands roamed over her body as though she was the most familiar territory he'd ever known. Savoring the way she moved and wriggled beneath his touch, he lingered on her hips and reached around to cup her firm bottom. He squeezed her tight and pulled her closer to him until he could feel Shay's flesh on every possible part of his body.

After lowering herself to the ground, Shay pulled Clint down on top of her and began tugging his clothes off. "I feel like my head's spinning," she said while leaning back to take in the sight of the endless blanket of stars.

Pulling her dress over her head, Clint couldn't bring himself to look away from Shay's naked body. Her little, erect nipples stood straight up on top of her pert breasts. Her stomach rose and fell with the quick pattern of her breath as her legs worked their way around his waist.

As his hands traced down the front of her body, Shay closed her eyes and arched her back, languidly moving her arms over her head. When she felt his finger slip between her legs, she bit down on one of her fingers and moaned under her breath.

172

Clint slowly felt inside the hot, moist lips between Shay's thighs. He then slid in another finger and left them there as he leaned down to lick the pink flesh surrounding the opening. Flicking his tongue in and out, Clint tasted her sensitive flesh until Shay lifted her hips up to grind against his face. As soon as he slid his fingers out, Shay reached down to grab his wrist.

"How do I taste?" she asked while pulling Clint's hand to her mouth. Shay's tongue extended until she could lick the tip of his fingers, sampling the juices that coated his skin. Smiling wickedly, she ran her tongue over her lips. "Mmmmm. Sweet."

"Yes," Clint said as he kicked his pants completely off and rose up above her. "You most certainly are."

Clint moved so that he was kneeling between Shay's open legs. She leaned back and shook her hair over her shoulders, making a little purring noise as she lifted her hips until the tip of his penis was pushing inside of her. With a slow, solid thrust, Clint plunged deeply into her and didn't stop until a louder moan came from the back of her throat.

Not caring who was around or what they could hear, Shay laid back onto the ground and clenched her legs tightly around Clint's waist. She reached out with one hand to rake her nails down his chest and used the other one to stroke his shaft as it glided in and out of her wet pussy.

Clint could feel the wind wrapping around his body as Shay's legs came to a rest on his shoulders. The chill in the air added another sensation to the numerous others that coursed wildly through his entire system. Every muscle in his body strained with the effort of pumping between her thighs.

Soon, she squirmed away from him and got onto her knees. Once there, she reached out to run her fingers through his hair, kissing his lips with a burning intensity. Their naked bodies pressed together, his almost penetrating hers as his rigid cock rubbed between her legs. Once again, she reached down to stroke him, moving the tip of his penis over her moist lips.

Before he could move inside of her, however, Clint felt

her body pull away. Shay turned her back to him and dropped down on all fours, raising her tight little bottom in the air and shaking it back in forth invitingly. Not one to pass up such a warm welcome, Clint grabbed her buttocks and rubbed them until he could hear the woman's familiar pleasured sounds.

First, Clint rubbed his fingertips over the sloping curve of her bottom. Then he gently traced along the pink lips of her vagina and spread them open just enough for him to fit inside. When his cock slipped inside, he held it there for a few moments, savoring the heat of her body.

But Shay wasn't so patient and she began moving back to take in more of him, clawing at the ground like a wild cat. Clint held onto her hips and thrust into her body, causing her to grunt with satisfaction. He thrust again and again, building up until their bodies were pounding together in a steady rhythm.

Clint looked down at the line of Shay's back as it sloped downward with a smooth, gentle curve that led all the way to her blonde hair, an unruly mess atop her head. Shay was laying with the side of her face pressed to the cold desert floor, her arms reaching out to grab desperate handfuls of the earth. The smile on her face was made of pure lust and the noises she made were almost ecstatic growls.

When Clint buried his entire length deep inside of her, Shay bit down on her lip and her entire body began to shake. Her growls had become stifled cries that could only be held back by every bit of self-control she could muster. All Clint had to do was pull out just a bit and then push in deeply once again to push her over the edge, sending her into a silent rage as the pleasure surged uncontrollably through her flesh.

Just seeing her was enough to bring Clint to that same point and when he felt his own climax coming, he began thrusting into her with increasing speed until the whole world seemed to blink out of existence, leaving nothing but him and Shay. Her vagina gripped his shaft as her orgasm swept through her, giving Clint a last burst of pleasure that sent bright streaks of color across his eyes.

It was only after the waves subsided that Clint realized

he'd had his eyelids clamped shut so hard, When he opened them again, the bits of color stayed for a few seconds before slowly fading away.

"Oh god, Clint," Shay whispered. "That was incredible."

All Clint could do after pulling out of her was drop back onto the ground and look up at the stars. After a few seconds, he said, "I . . . don't think I could move now if my life depended on it."

Shay crawled up beside him and lay down with her head resting on his chest. She draped one arm over his stomach and slid the other beneath his head. "I don't care who finds us like this. I just want to fall asleep right here next to you."

As much as Clint wanted to get up and get ready for the next day, he simply couldn't bring himself to budge. Instead, he took Shay in his arms and let the warmth of her skin protect him from the chill in the air.

Sleep took them both within seconds.

When Shay awoke, the sun was out and the fire was nothing but an ashen memory written in a few charred hunks of wood and a circle of stones. At first, she started reaching for Clint, but then another realization struck her.

She could see the campfire. She could also see Paul and Ellis stretched out on the ground not ten feet away.

Looking down, she realized she was in her slip and wrapped in one of the blankets Clint had taken from his saddlebag. Still a little confused, she sat up while holding the blanket to cover herself and looked around for Clint.

He was nowhere to be found.

Thinking back, Shay remembered some dream she'd had where Clint had picked her up and carried her away. That must have really happened, although she hadn't been conscious enough to say anything about it.

Judging by the position of the sun, it must have been somewhere around nine or ten o'clock. Shay found her dress folded up neatly beside her and quickly threw it on. Just as she made herself presentable, the other two began stirring in their spots. "Where's Clint?" she asked before the other two had even been given a chance to rub their eyes.

Paul was the first to shake off the effect of sleep and figure out what she was talking about. "He's got to be around here somewhere. Is he . . . ?"

Hearing the troubled tone in Paul's voice, Shay quickly shook her head. "There's no sign of him, or anybody else, for that matter."

Ellis stretched his arms up over his head and pointed toward Paul's horse. "He must'a left before we got up," the old man said. "His horse ain't even here, either."

Shay and Paul looked and found that Ellis was right.

It was at that moment that Shay knew what had happened. "We need to get moving," she said. "Hopefully, we can get to Ander's Valley before Clint tries to take on too many of them without us."

FORTY-TWO

Clint had gotten himself up and moving just before dawn. His senses never stopped searching for any trace of Tannen and his men, which was why he'd been waken up by the low rumble of approaching horses. With the others so tired that they were almost dead to the world, Clint didn't have any trouble at all getting himself around and moving Shay to the remains of the campfire behind the cluster of rocks.

Minutes later, he was dressed and on Eclipse's back, circling around to the other side of the trail and then breaking into a full gallop once he was certain the other gunmen had spotted him. He rode fast enough so that they would risk losing sight of him if they broke off to hunt for the others. Besides, from this distance, Clint doubted they could tell that he was the only one on the trail ahead of them.

His heart thumped inside his chest like a restless animal beating on the door of its cage. The nervousness only got worse the closer the riders behind him got to where Shay, Ellis and Paul were truly hiding. Clint slowed up just enough for him to be able to see Tannen's men whenever he stopped to look over his shoulder.

For a while, Clint was certain it sounded like some of the riders had broken away from chasing him. The more he thought about it, the worse Clint felt for taking such a terrible gamble with the others' lives. He pulled Eclipse to a stop at the crest of a small ridge and waited intently to spot the ones that had been chasing him. As more time passed, Clint expected to see some of the gunmen leading Paul's horse behind them. He even began waiting for the gunshots that would sound off during their execution at the hands of Barstow's men.

But then, after waiting for less than two minutes, Clint saw a group of riders come down the trail well past the small cluster of rocks. By the sound of it, there were just as many now as there were when he'd first heard them coming. Letting them get even closer, Clint was able to make out a few more details, which was enough to convince him that Paul's horse was not riding among them.

They must have only taken a few seconds to examine the tracks left by Eclipse before moving past the campsite. Just to be sure, Clint allowed them to get even closer as he closed his eyes and concentrated on the sound their horses' hooves made against the desert floor.

He was sure of it. All the riders he'd heard before were still coming after him.

Shay, Ellis and Paul were safe. At least . . . for the moment.

Thanking the Lord above that the riskiest part of his plan had worked, Clint turned Eclipse back toward Ander's Valley and snapped the reins. It was instinct more than anything else that told him he'd been spotted by the others and was once again in their sights.

He thought about all that had been going on over the last several days and nodded grimly to himself. It felt good to only be concerned with himself for the time being. And it would feel even better to put all of this business to rest once and for all.

It was time to stack the deck in his favor for a change.

Ander's Valley was a large town that was split into two distinct parts. The first looked to be the oldest and was mainly a collection of small stores and several homes. The second was a wider variety of businesses and even more houses that seemed to have sprung up around a newly built railroad depot.

It was to that depot that Clint rode without slowing Eclipse down more than was absolutely necessary. He made sure to steer around people crossing the street or big wagons, but even those were just barely enough to break the stallion's stride. Clint knew he had very little time to work. If things went the way he figured they would, however, he wouldn't need that much time.

He arrived at the train station and jumped down from the saddle as soon as Eclipse thundered to a halt. Not even bothering to tie the horse to one of the nearby posts, Clint rushed straight toward the large building and quickly found the telegraph office.

"I need to send a telegram," Clint said to the slight young man sitting behind the counter wearing a black vest and shirtsleeves.

"Where to?"

"Modillo."

The man nodded and plucked the pencil that had been stashed behind his right ear. Tearing off a piece of paper from a nearby ledger, he licked the tip of the pencil and said, "Whenever you're ready."

Tannen whipped his brown mare as though it had committed a crime. Not wanting to lose sight of Adams again, he didn't even bother to look and see if his men were behind him. He'd seen that familiar stallion on the trail that led to town and had been chasing it ever since. His men thought they'd found tracks leading to a camp, but once Tannen had spotted Adams, the chase had been on and it hadn't let up until they'd been separated at the edge of town.

Focusing on trying to pick up any sign of which way Adams had gone, Tannen nearly ran straight into the side of a stagecoach that rumbled around the corner directly in front of him. He pulled back on the reins, almost causing the horse to rear, just in time to avoid a collision.

As he swore loudly at the coach driver, Tannen could hear his men coming up alongside of him.

"I swear to Jesus Christ that if I lose Adams because of

this asshole, I'll shoot that driver in the face and use his coach for firewood," Tannen raged.

The man to Tannen's left, a killer by the name of Haskell, waited until his boss simmered down a bit before attracting any attention. "Even if the rest of them three was with Adams, they could have all gone in separate directions. They might already be hiding by now."

Wildly looking down the street and back and forth between every storefront, Tannen said, "It doesn't matter where the hell those others got to. All we need is to find Adams."

"Then you're in luck," came a voice from behind the men on horseback.

Tannen and his cowboys brought their mounts around to get a look at who'd just spoken to them. When they saw who it was, their hands went straight for their guns, but they stopped before clearing leather.

Clint didn't even flinch when he saw the reaction he'd caused. "You wanted me here so badly, then this is your lucky day. Of course," he said as he squared his shoulders and moved his hand toward the Colt at his side, "you might not think so in a couple of seconds."

FORTY-THREE

By the time Tannen and his men dropped down from their horses, everyone who'd been standing on or near the street had found some cover to hide behind. Clint stood in his spot and watched them without so much as a glimmer of expression on his face. Instead, he listened as the town seemed to empty out around him and then focused in on the four men standing less than fifteen feet away.

Wearing the dirty smile of a card cheat with an ace up his sleeve, Tannen took a couple strutting steps forward and locked eyes with Clint. "You ready to die, Adams?"

"Hadn't really thought about it."

"What's the matter? You blind? Can't you see all these guns that're about to go off in your direction? In case you didn't know, Barstow's got men in this town, too. If we need them, I just snap my fingers"—which Tannen did dramatically—"and they'll fill the air with lead."

Clint took a moment to look at each one of the men in turn. Despite what had just been said, there was still just Tannen and his three cowboys lined up like cans on a fence. "I've given you boys plenty of chances," he said. "You know where you stand with me. All I'll say now is that if you draw, you'll die. There's other towns to live in, so if you want to keep breathing, I suggest you find one. I think you've more than worn out your welcome here."

A dry breeze whipped down the street, heated by the sun

and crackling with the bad intentions of the men standing in its embrace. For the moment, Tannen didn't quite know how to react. Looking around, he couldn't see anyone else but his own men. All the locals had gone inside or made themselves scarce.

"You expect me to be scared of you?" Tannen shouted.

By way of response, Clint simply stared ahead. His hand held steady over his gun and his eyes remained fixed.

Tannen looked back at his men and then at Clint. "You're only one man. I don't care how fast you are, you're only one against four."

Clint still didn't say a word.

"All right," Tannen said, steeling himself. "On my count, boys . . . shoot this man down. Make it good and messy just like Mister Barstow ordered. One . . . two . . ."

"Three," Clint finished.

Two of Tannen's men were the first to draw and they got their pistols halfway out of their holsters before Clint even started to move. Two shots rang out in quick succession, but they sounded before either of the cowboys could pull their triggers. One bullet caught a man in the chest and sent him flying straight back to land flat on the ground, while the other carved a hole clean through the second one's head. That cowboy stood up for a second, blinking rapidly as all of his thoughts drained out of the back of his skull.

Seeing this, Tannen and his last remaining gunman, Haskell, ran for cover between two of the nearby buildings. Their feet kicked up a small dust cloud and carried them off as the body with the hollow head toppled over sideways.

Clint held the smoking Colt at hip level, watching steely-eyed as the other two men scampered off for one of the alleys. He waked slowly after them, stepping over the two fresh corpses and kicking their guns beneath the boardwalk.

It had all happened so quickly that Tannen barely got a chance to think. One moment he was getting ready to add a famous notch to his belt and the next his men were dropping dead and he was running away like a scolded dog. Now that he'd had a chance to get his wits back, he turned to Haskell and shoved the other man toward the street.

"We can still take him," Tannen insisted. "He's still just one man!"

But Haskell wasn't listening. His eyes and ears were open, but his brain was somewhere else. Glancing down at his hand, he almost seemed surprised that he still had a hold of his gun.

That was when they heard the footsteps.

Tannen threw himself down the alley just in time to see Clint come walking in from the street. Haskell stepped out as well, but it was hard to tell what, if anything, that one was thinking.

"Last chance, Adams," Tannen said. "You can—"

"Shut your mouth and finish what you started."

Clint's words struck both men like cold hammers right between their eyes. In that instant, Tannen and Haskell knew they could probably get out alive if they gave up. But then, both of them looked to one another and nodded.

Tannen's gun felt heavy in his hand, but he raised it anyway. Seeing this, Haskell followed suit and brought up his pistol, hoping that if they fired as fast as they could, perhaps some of their bullets would cut Adams down.

Gunshots echoed down the alley like rolling thunder and smoke billowed out to drift into the cramped space. First one shot and then another ripped through the air, causing all the faces that watched from behind their cover to twitch and turn away. From all the windows of both buildings and from either end of the alley itself, locals did their best to get a good view without putting themselves into the line of fire.

Fighting to keep his hand steady, Tannen felt as though the lead was turning slowly in space rather than whipping from the sparks and smoke to tear through flesh and bone. His palms were sweaty on his gun and he could somehow hear his heart beating wildly in his chest.

Clint's mind was completely attuned to what he needed to do. He thought about Sarah's sad, dead face and the misery of her surviving husband. He thought of all the frightened citizens of these three towns and how they'd been robbed of their freedom of choice to live the way they wanted.

As his finger tightened around his trigger, Clint blinked

once and then again as two more shots exploded from his Colt.

Haskell dropped first, his upper chest punctured by two rounds. He spun on one foot and sent his gun flying into a stack of crates piled up along one side of the alley. The man's last breath left him when he hit the ground on his chest, exposing a back covered in fresh blood.

Tannen squeezed his trigger again and again, gritting his teeth to force his way through the sharp pain that had started lancing through his body. He'd killed so many, that he didn't see any reason why he couldn't do one more. After that, he could take out his celebrations and frustrations on this town. He'd show them their new boss.

He fired until he couldn't fire any more. But then he realized that the gun in his hand hadn't even been cocked yet. Its hammer was still resting against his thumb and not one round had gone off.

The firing he'd done was all in his mind. Somehow, what he'd wanted to do had gotten mixed up with what he'd actually done. He was seeing things. Tannen had heard about this happening to men who'd been starving or lost in the desert. It also happened to men when they were dying.

Looking down at himself, Tannen quickly discovered which one applied to him. He could see one black hole in the center of his chest. Then . . . he couldn't see much of anything because of the flow of blood running over his eyes.

Tannen replayed the battle in his head a hundred more times before he finally hit the dirt. Every other time, he was the victorious one. And then . . . it all . . . went . . . black. . . .

FORTY-FOUR

Clint stepped into the middle of the street and emptied out all six of his empty shell casings. Tannen and all of his men had drawn on him, which was exactly what he'd wanted to happen. He needed them to have a better than average chance in order to leave the correct impression. What he hadn't quite planned on was the fact that his own Colt had been the only gun fired in the exchange.

"These men belonged to Matt Barstow," Clint said loudly to any and all of the bystanders. "These were his best shooters. If he comes around here, I want you all to remember this day. Know that he doesn't have anything to throw at you but empty threats. And if he tries to threaten any of you," he added after reloading his gun and snapping it back into his holster, "ride him out on a rail."

He then turned and walked back to where he'd left Eclipse. Riled up from all the commotion, the Darley Arabian wanted to break into a run, but Clint made sure he left town at his own leisurely pace.

Nobody said a word to him until he was almost out of Ander's Valley. It was an old woman who did the talking. She had her silvery hair tied back into a bun and she propped herself up using an gnarled wooden cane.

"We knew those men," she said. "Thank you so much for what you done."

185

Clint nodded to her and continued riding. He knew Shay would still need a ride back into civilization.

Barstow had started to grow impatient after he hadn't heard the day's report from Tannen. Just as he was about to let his impatience fester into rage, a knock sounded on his office door.

"Come in," he said.

His youthful assistant poked his head inside and held out a folded piece of paper. "Telegram came for you, sir."

"Excellent. Give it here."

The message read: YOUR MEN WON'T BE LEAVING AN-DER'S VALLEY. STOP. IT'S JUST YOU AND ME NOW. STOP. FIND SOMEWHERE ELSE TO LIVE AND DON'T GIVE ME AN EXCUSE TO TRACK YOU DOWN. STOP.

C. ADAMS

Barstow got a good laugh from that which lasted all day long . . . right up to the point when he got word from one of his last employees in Ander's Valley who hadn't skipped town just yet. There was nothing that Barstow heard that made him laugh that time. In fact, he left Modillo the next morning without so much as a word of explanation.

A month after that, folks stopped asking where he'd gone. They were too busy electing a new sheriff.

Watch for

PLAYING FOR BLOOD

241st novel in the exciting GUNSMITH series
from Jove

Coming in January!

J. R. ROBERTS
THE GUNSMITH